Commit thy way unto the Lord; trust also in him;
and he shall bring it to pass.

—*Psalm* 37:5

For my sweet nieces:
Kingsley, Reagan, Layla and Aurelia.

"Yes, boss, I'll help you pack."

Cassie rolled her eyes. "When are you going to knock it off with all the boss nonsense?"

Devin pretended to think about it. "Maybe when you're no longer my boss."

"You know we don't have a hierarchy here."

"Well," he said, lips twitching, "that may be true, but I was always taught to respect my elders."

Immediately, from the look on her face, Devin could tell that he'd pushed it too far. "Sorry, Cass. I'm just kidding."

He was twenty-seven, and if he remembered correctly, her thirtieth birthday would have taken place recently. Three years had been a big gap when they were in school, but not now.

"Of course I'll help you pack. It would be pretty uncharitable of me to say no after everything you've been doing for Hailey."

She waved that off. "I love doing things with Hailey."

"And she loves doing things with you." He was hopeful that the close proximity meant Cassie would continue to be a friend, mentor and role model to his little girl.

As long as he didn't do anything to mess it up.

Meghann Whistler grew up in Canada but spent her summers on the beaches of Cape Cod. When she's not reading, writing or jamming out to Christian rock music, you can find her enjoying a relaxing evening with her rocket scientist husband (seriously—he's a real, live rocket scientist!) or playing with her three kids. She loves to hear from her readers, who can reach her at meghannwhistler.com.

Books by Meghann Whistler

Love Inspired

Falling for the Innkeeper
The Baby's Christmas Blessing
Their Unlikely Protector
The Pastor's Hope
Trusting the Single Dad

Visit the Author Profile page at LoveInspired.com.

TRUSTING THE SINGLE DAD

MEGHANN WHISTLER

LOVE INSPIRED
INSPIRATIONAL ROMANCE

MIX
Paper | Supporting responsible forestry
FSC® C021394
www.fsc.org

LOVE INSPIRED®
INSPIRATIONAL ROMANCE

ISBN-13: 978-1-335-52915-2

Recycling programs for this product may not exist in your area.

Trusting the Single Dad

For questions and comments about the quality of this book, please contact us at CustomerService@Harlequin.com.

Love Inspired
22 Adelaide St. West, 41st Floor
Toronto, Ontario M5H 4E3, Canada
www.LoveInspired.com

HarperCollins Publishers
Macken House, 39/40 Mayor Street Upper,
Dublin 1, D01 C9W8, Ireland
www.HarperCollins.com

Printed in Lithuania

1 2 3 4 5 6 7 8 9 10 LIT 28 27 26 25

Chapter One

Cassie Reed's day had started off rocky, and it just kept going downhill.

Her foster baby, Tyler, was teething, and he'd been up at least ten times during the night. She'd rock him back to sleep and lay him in his crib, only for him to start howling again a mere half hour later.

All. Night. Long.

And now, of course, he was sound asleep in his car seat, which she'd placed on the floor of Aunt Mirriam's living room, while she was barely coherent. She might be experiencing exhaustion-induced brain fog, too, because she was having trouble making sense of the declaration her aunt had just made.

Looking back and forth between her aunt, her two brothers and interloper Devin Spencer, she gave her head an adamant shake. "No. No way."

"Cassandra," her aunt said, her voice rife with disappointment. In jeans and a red V-neck T-shirt, Aunt Mirriam looked a lot like an off-duty, off-season Mrs. Claus.

If the fictional Mrs. Claus ever got frustrated, that was, which Cassie was certain she did not.

A twinge of guilt pulled at her—she hated disappointing people—but she resolutely pushed it away. Aunt Mirriam had disappointed her first! When she'd pitched the idea of Cassie, Jonah and Alex taking over the summer camp she and Uncle

Vince used to run here in Sandpiper Cove, Cape Cod, she hadn't said one word about Devin Spencer joining the team.

No, she'd waited until today, when they were supposed to sign the paperwork, to spring his involvement on them.

"Why is this the first we're hearing about it?" Cassie demanded.

"Don't blame your aunt." Devin splayed his hands in a placating gesture. "She didn't know I needed a new job until yesterday."

Cassie flicked her gaze to the man who, as a child, had been her brother Jonah's best friend. He had nice hands, she'd give him that. Must be from all the swimming he did as the aquatics program director over at the Chatsworth Country Club.

He also had gray eyes, a big nose and a crooked smile that spelled trouble with a capital *T*.

Well, she wasn't getting dragged back into troubled waters anytime soon, thank you very much. She'd spent enough time there already with her ex-husband. No way was she putting herself through that again, even if it was only on the job.

"What happened?" she challenged. "You get fired?"

"Actually—" he ran a hand through his dark, slightly mussed hair "—yeah, I did."

"Oh." Cassie could have kicked herself. She was never rude. "I'm sorry."

Devin shrugged.

"Dude," Jonah said from his seat on the couch. "When did this happen?"

"Last week."

Her brother's eyes popped. "Why?"

Again, Devin lifted his shoulder, but the fiery expression on his face spoke much louder than the careless gesture ever could. "Turns out nepotism is alive and well."

"Charles fired you and gave the job to Lucas?" Jonah asked, incredulous. "Didn't you train that kid?"

Devin nodded, a storm roiling in his eyes.

Aunt Mirriam's brow creased. "I thought Lucas was studying business."

"He was," Devin confirmed.

"Did he fail to graduate?"

"Oh, he graduated, all right. Then he bummed around Europe for eight or nine months."

"And what makes him qualified to take over your job at the country club?" Aunt Mirriam asked.

"Beats me," Devin said, bitterness threaded through his tone. "But why work your way up from the bottom when you can inherit a seat at the top?"

Then he stopped and closed his eyes for a second, exhaling heavily before adding, "Sorry, guys. I need to do a better job of turning this over. Clearly, I'm still struggling with the situation."

"Of course you are, honey." Aunt Mirriam gave his hand a brisk pat. "Anybody would be."

"It was such a great setup for me and Hailey." Devin's daughter, Hailey, was in first grade, and from what Cassie had heard, she'd practically grown up at the country club. "Free childcare is an employee benefit that's hard to beat."

"Well," Aunt Mirriam said, "we'll do our level best to make sure you're both taken care of."

Jonah and Alex nodded their agreement while Cassie gaped at them.

Was she the only one who wasn't on board with this? Who felt blindsided?

The shock was almost as bad as it had been the day Jared told her he wanted a divorce.

Cassie might have been powerless to stop the divorce, but she could absolutely take her power back here and now.

She turned to her aunt. "Is this a done deal? Because if you give Devin a job at Camp Piper, I'm out."

"Cassie!" Jonah and Aunt Mirriam protested in unison.

"Devin's a lifeguard, Cass," Alex said mildly. "His skills'll come in handy."

"Plus, he's good with a hammer," Jonah added. Devin scoffed, and Jonah shot him a quelling look. "Bro, you know it's true." Then he aimed his gaze at Cassie. "We worked together on a couple of Habitat for Humanity projects back in high school. The extra muscle will come in handy for restoring all the cabins." The elements had done a good job of chipping away at them over the past few years while the camp sat empty, and they needed a lot of work.

Still, though. Still!

Cassie frowned at Jonah before turning back to Aunt Mirriam. "I thought we were going to do this as a family. Not the four of us—" she gestured between her aunt and her brothers "—plus some rando off the street."

Devin snorted. "You've known me since I was five years old. I'm hardly a random guy off the street."

"I know that I've driven you home from parties where you were too drunk to see straight, let alone walk in a straight line." She'd always been the responsible older sister, and when Jonah had told her that his friend was in trouble, she hadn't hesitated to drop everything and hop in the car.

Thing was, it hadn't been once. It hadn't been twice. It had been at least once a month her whole senior year of high school…when Devin was just fourteen years old.

A person didn't simply grow out of a problem like that.

Cassie knew, because her ex-husband had been a drinker, too, although his drinking had gotten much worse after—

No. She wrenched her mind away from the circumstances that had led to the acceleration of Jared's drinking. Away from his immaturity, his self-centeredness, his lies. *You're not going there right now.*

"That was a long time ago," Devin countered. "I've got

Hailey now. I haven't touched a drop of alcohol since before she was born."

She opened her mouth to reply, but Tyler woke up and immediately started screaming.

Cassie sighed heavily as she knelt down and unclipped him from his car seat, then stood and popped him up on her shoulder, bouncing him and patting his back in an attempt to calm him down.

He was six months old, and at his last checkup he'd weighed in at a hefty eighteen pounds. She'd definitely noticed that her arms had gotten more toned as he'd grown bigger—a benefit she'd never anticipated before she'd taken him in. "Shh, shh, shh," she crooned. "You're okay."

In response, he cried harder.

"Is he hungry?" Aunt Mirriam asked.

Cassie shook her head. He was on a feeding schedule, and he was used to getting a bottle five times a day. "Teething."

"Oh, poor baby." Aunt Mirriam clutched her hands to her heart.

"Does he take a pacifier?" Devin asked.

"I've tried, but he doesn't like them. He'll suck his thumb, but not when he's worked up like this."

"Hailey never liked pacifiers, either." Then he held out his hands. "Want me to hold him?"

She was tempted to say no on principle, but at the same time, she needed to search her diaper bag for Tyler's teething ring. "You don't mind?"

"Not at all," he said, using those strong, capable hands of his to lift the boy into his arms. "Hey, buddy, what's going on? What's wrong? Your teeth hurt?"

Tyler's cries slowed as he registered that Devin was a completely new-to-him person. He hiccupped a few times, reached out with one of his chubby baby hands and patted Devin on the cheek, then balled up his little fist and bopped him on the nose.

Cassie stifled a smile. If that didn't tell you the kid was meant to be hers, nothing would.

Devin chuckled, plucking the boy's hand from his face and relocating it to his shoulder. "Easy there, kiddo. I don't need a broken nose on top of everything else. And you're a bruiser, aren't you? I can tell you've been eating well." He threw a glance at Cassie. "What's his name?"

"Tyler."

"Tyler, I'm Devin. You want to go outside for a minute, say hello to Hailey?" Again, he glanced at Cassie. "You don't mind, do you?"

"Uh…no." She'd been rooted to the spot, watching their easy interaction. How many times during her marriage had she daydreamed about a scene almost exactly like this? "Go ahead."

He strode out the door with Tyler, and Cassie shook her head as she dug into the diaper bag. Daydreaming about Devin Spencer's paternal qualities? As if.

Alex laughed. "Guy's a baby whisperer. Who knew?"

"I did," Aunt Mirriam said staunchly. "That man is a wonderful father."

"Yeah, but it's different with your own kid," Jonah said, "or so I've heard. For him to have the magic touch with Tyler? It's worth keeping him around just for that."

Cassie frowned. Tyler wasn't usually a difficult baby. Yes, there had definitely been an adjustment period at first, but they were well past that now. She certainly didn't need to entertain the idea of working with Devin Spencer just so he could help her with the baby.

Blocking out her family's chatter, she dumped the contents of the diaper bag on the ground. Frankly, she was still mad at the lot of them. And Tyler's teething ring was nowhere to be found.

Huffing, she shot an accusatory look at Jonah. "Was hiring him your idea?"

"No, but you've got to admit it's genius. We need someone in charge of water safety since the cabins are right on the pond and the camp's so close to the beach."

"But it's—he's—"

"He's not a kid anymore, Cass," Jonah said softly. "Give him a chance."

She shoved a few of the items that she'd dumped out of the diaper bag back inside. "You can't spring something like this on me and expect me to be okay with it."

"I'm sorry you're upset," Aunt Mirriam said, "but you know how your uncle felt about lending a helping hand. And when the person who needs help has the exact skills you're looking for? That's a God thing, for sure."

Cassie dropped the diapers she was holding back into the bag and rubbed her temples. It couldn't be a God thing. It just couldn't. She didn't want it to be.

No, what she wanted was to run this camp with her brothers—men she knew, men she trusted, men she felt safe with. Asking her to trust a man who'd proven unreliable in the past was a step too far.

After all, she'd trusted Jared and look what that had cost her: almost a decade of her life she'd never get back. And unfortunately, that wasn't the worst of it. Not even close. "I need some time to think about this."

"That's fine, honey." Aunt Mirriam gave her an encouraging smile. "Take all the time you need."

"And I need to get a new teething ring for Tyler. I don't know where the other one went."

"Why don't you run down to the drugstore and grab one right now? I'm sure that between everyone here, we can keep Tyler happy until you get back."

She didn't love the idea of leaving Tyler behind, but she

had to admit she could use a little break. Aunt Mirriam lived on Warbler Lane, so it would be an easy walk to the drugstore on Plover Street, Sandpiper Cove's main hub for shopping and restaurants. "Okay," she said. "I'll be quick."

Stepping outside, Cassie inhaled deeply. She loved springtime on Cape Cod. After following Jared to Houston while he was finishing med school, then to Los Angeles for his residency and finally back to Boston, where they'd met when she was a first-year nursing student, she was happy to be home, despite the circumstances of her divorce. The air in Sandpiper Cove was cleaner, the pace of life slower and more conducive to putting faith and family first.

Of course, as soon as she'd moved back, her parents had left on a year-long, around-the-world cruise. They'd worked hard and saved for it for years, and although Cassie missed them, she didn't begrudge them the experience. And she truly was happy to be closer to Aunt Mirriam and her brothers, even though she was annoyed with all three of them today.

On the front lawn, Devin had Tyler in his lap. Hailey, a cutie with messy brown hair and a gap-toothed smile, was sitting across from them, trying to teach Tyler how to play pattycake. It was March, so it wasn't warm yet, but Hailey had shed her puffy pink jacket and left it in a little pile on the grass.

"I'm going to pop over to the store," Cassie called out to Devin. "If he gets fussy, bring him inside to Aunt Mirriam."

"You got it, boss." He flashed her a grin and a thumbs-up.

The boss moniker—and his self-satisfied grin—irritated her all over again. It was like he *knew* he was going to win the standoff they had going on right now about hiring him to help at the camp.

Cassie rolled her shoulders a few times and sighed. The most irritating part about it was that he was probably right. If she wanted to have a real shot at adopting Tyler, she needed the security and stability that would come with running—and, after this first season, co-owning—Camp Piper.

And she wanted to adopt Tyler more than anything else in the world.

She'd always dreamed of becoming a mother, and for a while there, it hadn't looked like it was ever going to happen. The fact that it was happening now, after her divorce, was definitely not the way she'd planned it, but God was funny like that.

Is this whole curveball with Devin Spencer part of your plan, too, Lord? If so, gotta tell you, I'm not laughing.

She hit the drugstore, bought three teething rings and headed back to Aunt Mirriam's.

As she drew closer, she saw Hailey doing cartwheels on the edge of the lawn; Devin must have taken Tyler back inside. The girl hadn't spotted her, so Cassie stopped to watch and smiled, remembering herself at that age: joyful. Spontaneous. Unreserved.

When Hailey straightened, she yelled, "Two, four, six, eight, who do we appreciate? Dad! Dad! Daaaaaaad!" Then she flung her arms into the air and one of her bracelets glinted in the sun as it flew off her wrist and into the street.

Without looking, she gasped and sprang forward to retrieve it.

"Stop!" Cassie screamed as she leaped forward, too, because she *had* looked and seen the SUV barreling too fast down her aunt's residential street.

The SUV's tires squealed as Cassie slammed into the little girl, pushing her out of the way a split second before the SUV's bumper thumped into her left side, sending a searing shot of agony through her as her whole body was flung onto the hood of the car.

Then—amidst a riot of pain and fear and the scent of burning rubber—she cracked her head on the windshield and blacked out.

* * *

"Daddy," Hailey whispered, worry making her little voice wobble, "is she dead?"

"No, silly pants," Devin rushed to reassure her, "she's just taking a nap. Like I told you, she hurt her knee and bumped her head yesterday, which is why she had to stay here at Ms. Mirriam's house last night after they let her out of the hospital instead of going back to her own place."

"But why's she so sleepy? Only babies take naps in the afternoon!"

Cassie's lips tipped up into a smile as she cracked her eyes open, then struggled to sit up straight on Mirriam's living room sofa. "You'd be tired, too, cutie, if you were forced to sleep on this lumpy couch all night long."

So she *did* still have a sense of humor. Good to know. After yesterday, Devin hadn't been sure.

From the moment he'd started taking a romantic interest in girls, he'd thought Cassie—with her shiny brown hair, gold-flecked eyes and cover-girl smile—was the full package: smart, beautiful, helpful and kind. He'd spent many an hour as a young teenager wishing he were three or four years older so he'd have a shot with Cassandra Reed.

Unfortunately, his reckless behavior back then had torpedoed any shot he might have had with her now. Romantically, or even as a friend. A colleague.

And since he desperately needed the job at Camp Piper, he had to see if he could at least start making things right.

He pushed Hailey forward a few inches. "Hailey has something she'd like to say to you."

"Thank you for saving my life," his daughter said earnestly, lisping the "s" sound due to her missing front teeth. "I will never, ever, ever run into the street without looking ever again!"

"I'm glad to hear that," Cassie replied solemnly. "I'm sure you know now that it's very dangerous."

Hailey nodded.

"Okay, peanut," Devin said, patting Hailey's shoulder. "Go see if Ms. Mirriam has a snack for you in the kitchen."

The girl's eyes lit up. "Can I have cookies?"

Devin nodded. He didn't normally let her have sugary snacks unless they were dessert after a meal, but he wasn't rigid about it if they were out and about with friends. "If Ms. Mirriam offers you some, you can go ahead."

His daughter squealed with excitement and dashed for the kitchen door.

Cassie smiled, watching her. "I'm so glad she didn't get hurt."

Understatement of the century.

Devin had been keeping it together pretty well today, but last night, his mind kept veering back to what might have happened if Cassie hadn't returned from the drugstore at the precise moment she had.

"I'm sorry I can't say the same for you." Thankfully, she'd woken up almost immediately after the crash, and she'd barely even had a concussion. Her knee, however, was a different story, as evidenced by the brace wrapped around it and the fact that she'd elevated it on the coffee table as soon as she'd sat up. "If you hadn't been there… I can't even…" He blew out a breath. "Thank you. From the bottom of my heart, Cassie. She's my world."

"I'm just glad she's okay. What was she chasing after? A bracelet?"

He gave his head a rueful shake. "That bracelet. Gift from her mother, who's not really in the picture. So, of course, that makes it even more valuable in Hailey's eyes."

"Aww. Poor thing. Did you find it?"

He sighed. "Yep. We took a look just now before we came

in. I'll need to take it to a jeweler to get it repaired. It'll probably cost more to get it fixed than the silly thing is worth."

"Why isn't Hailey's mom in the picture?"

Devin glanced at the kitchen door to confirm that his daughter wouldn't overhear him. "Let's just say I made a lot of bad decisions back in the day. But you already knew that. It's why you don't want me working at the camp, right?"

Over the past seven years, he'd gotten used to eating humble pie and proving to the people who'd known him as a teenager that he'd matured into a law-abiding, tax-paying, overprotective dad of a precocious little girl. What he wouldn't give, though, to have people like Cassie start giving him the benefit of the doubt.

She frowned and started to say something, but Hailey ran back into the room, her eyes bright with excitement. "Daddy! Daddy! Tyler just woke up! Ms. Mirriam's changing his diaper and then she's going to bring him in here! She said maybe I can hold him, and I really want to hold him! Can I?"

Devin glanced at Cassie, hoping she wouldn't mind. "You'll have to ask Miss Cassie."

"Can I? Can I, please, Miss Cassie?" Hailey pressed her hands together in supplication.

"Sure, sweetie," Cassie said, motioning toward the armchair in the corner with her chin. "Go sit down over there and Aunt Mirriam or your dad will hand him to you."

Hailey practically flew over to the chair. "Can he crawl yet?"

"Not yet."

"Can he talk?"

"Nope. But he likes to babble."

Hailey whipped her head in Devin's direction. "What's that?"

"When babies are talking, but they're not using real words," he said.

Her little forehead furrowed. "Did I do that?"

"You sure did."

"I wonder what I was saying."

"Wah! I'm hungry! Wah! I'm tired! Wah! I'm bored! Wah! Pick me up!"

"Dad!" She giggled. "That's silly!"

"You're silly!"

"Well, you're the silliest jelly bean in the box!" It was his signature line when they were teasing each other, and he laughed to hear her steal it.

"Knock knock," Mirriam interrupted their silly fest. "I have one sweet little boy here who's dying to see his mama."

When Tyler caught sight of Cassie, he started bouncing and squawking and kicking his little feet. "Yes, baby," Mirriam cooed. "She's right here. She's been waiting for you."

"Miss Cassie said I could hold him," Hailey announced.

Mirriam winked at her. "Let's give him a minute with his mama first, then we'll bring him over to you, Hailey Boo."

Devin watched as Mirriam handed Tyler to Cassie, whose face shone with tenderness as she covered the boy's face in kisses. His heart hitched, because it was exactly the expression he'd hoped to see on Shannon's face when Hailey was born.

But Shannon hadn't bonded with baby Hailey. She hadn't wanted to back then.

Or since, really, although every now and then she'd call or send a gift, getting Hailey's hopes up for weeks before they came crashing back down.

Now that Shannon had accepted a job in Boston starting this summer, Devin was worried about how much more often Hailey would be forced to ride that roller coaster of raised and dashed expectations. Even worse, he wondered if Shannon might ask for shared custody, or—God forbid—try to take Hailey away from him altogether.

That was just one of the many reasons he needed to nail

down a new job ASAP. He needed to scrape together enough money to hire a lawyer if worse came to worst and Shannon wanted to reassert her parental rights.

"Thank you for all your help last night," Cassie said to Mirriam.

"Of course, honey. Family helps family. I'm just glad you won't need knee surgery."

"I know." Cassie rolled her eyes. "Just weeks of wearing this brace and basically being useless."

"Well," Mirriam said, taking Tyler and handing him to Hailey, who beamed as the boy settled himself in her lap, "good thing you'll have Devin and Hailey to help you while you heal."

Devin's gaze shot to Cassie's face, but she didn't look surprised—or upset—about what her aunt had just said. "Uh… did I miss something?"

"Congrats," Cassie said wryly. "My aunt and I talked for a long time this morning, and because of this injury, I'm going to need a lot of help for the next few weeks. Since Jonah's still working at the school and Alex can't do any heavy lifting—" the older of her two younger brothers was a PE teacher at the local high school, and the younger had mobility issues due to cerebral palsy "—if you still want to be part of revamping and reopening Camp Piper, you're in. But," she added quickly, "it's just on a trial basis for now, and you've got to help me with Tyler, too."

Relief, hope and gratitude shot through him as fast as a tidal wave, and if Devin could have put his whole body into his grin, he would have. *Thank You, Lord.* So long as he proved himself during the trial period, he and Hailey wouldn't have to leave Sandpiper Cove. He could keep her in her current school and start saving up in case he needed to consult a child custody lawyer about the situation with Shannon.

"I don't know about that," he drawled, still smiling as he

glanced over to where Hailey had Tyler in her lap. “The two of you look like you’re going to be a lot of work.”

“Oh, buddy,” Cassie said, laughing, “you have absolutely no idea.”

Chapter Two

Devin held Tyler in his arms as he rammed his hip into the cabin door. It took a few tries to get it open. When Mirriam and Vince had built the camp more than two decades ago, they'd opted for traditional log cabins rather than cedar-shingled Cape Cod cottages. Regardless, the humidity, and the lack of upkeep over the last few years, had certainly taken a toll.

"Oof." The musty smell of mildew assaulted him as he stepped inside, and Hailey scrunched up her nose, too, as she followed him into the cabin's large, dormitory-style room.

"Pee-ew," his daughter said, waving a hand in front of her face.

"What?" Cassie asked from behind them, clamoring to get in on her crutches.

"It stinks." Devin stepped away from the door so she could maneuver her way in.

"Ugh, yeah. Take Tyler back outside. I don't want him getting sick from mold."

"Where do you want me to put him?" The camper cabins were situated around Piper Pond, one of the so-called "kettle ponds" formed by melting glaciers that dotted Cape Cod.

"I've got a blanket in the trunk of the car. You can lay that down on the grass and let him hang out there with Hailey." The cabins were about twenty feet back from the pond, just on the edge of the forest, so it would be extremely difficult for Tyler, who couldn't crawl, to get near the water.

Devin glanced at his daughter. "You hear that, peanut? You get to babysit."

"Yay!" she squealed as she ran back outside.

It was chilly out but Hailey was sufficiently bundled up, so he wasn't concerned. Devin retrieved the requested blanket and spread it out for the kids. Mirriam hadn't done much in the way of camp maintenance since Vince had passed away, but she'd never canceled the gardeners, so at least the place wasn't massively overgrown.

Piper Pond was about a half a mile inland from Piper Marsh, in the middle of a forest of scraggly pitch pine and oak trees. The oaks weren't budding just yet, but green moss was already starting to climb up the trunks of many of the trees, lending an earthy scent to the salty ocean breeze blowing in from the marsh.

Devin had never had the experience of being a camper here, but he couldn't wait to start planning out all the various activities they could do with the kids. Between the marsh, the forest, the pond and the beach, the possibilities were endless.

And the quiet here—the peace. He could understand why Mirriam had never wanted to sell it, despite the fact that the camp had been built on twenty-five acres of valuable coastal land.

It was a shame, though, that she'd let the buildings fall into such a state of disrepair.

"Don't let Tyler roll off the blanket," Devin instructed his daughter. "And don't go near the pond." Then he hurried back inside, where Cassie was making her way, on her crutches, down the aisle between two long rows of bunk beds.

"We're going to have to get rid of all these mattresses," she called out over her shoulder.

"No kidding."

"And there's a lot of dead bugs."

"Let's just hope there aren't any rodents."

She grimaced at him. "Ew."

"Don't worry, boss. I'll take the lead on cleaning everything up."

She gave him a wry look. "Cool it with the boss stuff, would you?"

He shot an amused glance right back at her. "Why? You are, in fact, my boss."

She just shook her head. "We're going to need mold control spray. Lots of it."

He nodded. "That's easy. They'll have plenty of that at the home improvement store. Are we starting in here, though?"

"No, we should go look at the director's cabin. It's on the other side of the dining hall and the campfire site. That's where Tyler and I are going to live. And if you and Hailey want to move onsite, you can have the nurse's cabin, which is right next door."

Whoa, Devin hadn't seen that coming. But how great would it be to stop paying rent? His lease was month-to-month at this point, so moving out wouldn't be a problem if that's what he decided to do. The only question was whether Cassie would want him to keep working here after her knee healed.

Despite his facetious tone, he hadn't been joking when he'd called her his boss. And bosses, as he knew from personal experience, didn't always have their employees' best interests in mind.

"Won't we need the nurse's cabin for, you know, the nurse?"

Cassie smirked. "Nope. You're looking at her."

His jaw dropped. He'd heard through the grapevine that she'd married a doctor, but he'd had no idea she'd become a nurse. He should have stayed in better touch with Jonah after high school. Hopefully, working together at Camp Piper would help him restore his relationship with his former best friend.

"You're a nurse? That's amazing. How come you're not working at a hospital or a doctor's office or something?"

"I quit my job in Boston to move back here after my divorce. I was looking for something local when I got the call about Tyler—"

"Wait," he said, shocked all over again. "Tyler's not your son?"

"Not yet. He's a foster child."

The more Devin learned about her, the more intrigued he became. "That's awesome. Good for you."

"Thanks," she said. "I've started an application to adopt him, but it's a slow process. And for the home study, we need to make sure the director's cabin is safe for him, physically."

"Ah, gotcha. So we've got our work cut out for us, huh?"

She glanced around the dank and dusty interior of the cabin. "Ya think?"

"So back to why you're going to be working here instead of at, say, Cape Cod Memorial Hospital?"

"Oh, that's easy. I wanted to be able to spend time with Tyler, so I stopped job hunting for a few months after I took him in. When Aunt Mirriam asked if we'd be interested in getting the camp going again, it seemed like serendipity. I loved this place growing up, and having the chance to bring it back to life with Tyler as my right-hand man is a dream. Where else am I going to find a job that lets me keep him with me all day?"

Devin nodded. "Sounds a lot like what attracted me to working at the country club. It was pretty great to have Hailey so close by during the workday. But working here is going to be great, too. This place is incredible. Your aunt and uncle couldn't have picked a better spot for a camp."

"I know! Just think about how much the kids will be able to learn about Cape Cod's ecology! We can take them bird-watching, fishing, digging for clams, looking for crabs. It's going to be so cool."

"And the forest looks like a fun place to explore, too."

"Yeah, we used to do a lot back there when I was a camper. Hiking, archery, survival skills, capture the flag. But first things first. We've got to get the cabins and the dining hall back in working order. Then we can do an audit of all the old amenities and see which ones we can rehab before the end of June."

Devin tapped his chin. He was a hard worker, but there was a lot to do to get this place up and running. "Do you really think we'll be able to open this summer?"

"That's the goal. My aunt's handling the licensing requirements, and Alex has already started interviewing potential counselors and other employees. So it's up to you and me to get the buildings back in shape as soon as possible. If we miss our summer deadlines, we'll just have to focus on recruiting school groups to come in the fall."

When Mirriam had pitched the camp to him, she'd mentioned that she and Vince used to run it year-round. "Does Mirriam still have her old contacts at the schools?"

"She does, and that's where she's going to spend some of her time while we're doing the manual labor."

"We?" he said, shooting a pointed glance at her busted knee.

Her cheeks pinked. "You, mostly."

The fact that he could make her blush filled his chest with an odd sort of satisfaction. Of course, her blush was born from embarrassment, not attraction, but still. There was a part of him that liked it. A lot.

Exactly the same as when he was a middle schooler, and the only time she'd pay attention to him was when he teased her.

Yeah, but you're not in middle school anymore, bucko, so cut it out.

He knew that the more he needled her, the less likely she'd

be to want him to continue working here past his trial period, so…he definitely needed to stop. "Are the school groups from around here?"

"Some, but most are from Boston and Providence. She and Uncle Vince also used to host church groups and organize family camps for low-income households and camps for foster kids, too."

"They were always good at giving back."

"Hopefully we can get that up and running sooner rather than later. Obviously, anything that helps foster kids is close to my heart."

"Sounds good to me." He'd been in survival mode for a long time, trying to provide a good life for Hailey, but he'd love to have the opportunity to give back to the community now. If he and Hailey really could move onsite, if he really could stop paying rent, that would open *a lot* of doors for him.

Cassie squinted at him. "How come you never came to camp here?"

He lifted his shoulder. "Couldn't afford it."

"They would have comped you."

"They tried to. My parents said no. Accepting handouts wasn't their thing." His parents had adopted him later in life, and they'd been quite…set in their ways. When he'd rebelled as a teenager, he'd rebelled hard, and the fact that his dad had passed away before he'd had a chance to make amends was one of the biggest regrets of his life.

He didn't like dwelling on it, though, so he moved on. "If you take the director's cabin and I take the nurse's cabin, where are Jonah and Alex going to stay?" In addition to the dining hall and the two aforementioned cabins, there were six large camper cabins: three for the boys and three for the girls.

"Alex won't live onsite," Cassie said. "He's mostly going to be behind the scenes, doing the accounting and the HR, so he won't need to be here for the day-to-day."

Devin tipped his head in assent. Given Alex's physical limitations, that made sense.

"Jonah's not sure yet. This summer, he'll probably act as a counselor and sleep in one of the boys' cabins. But after that, he might build one of his own."

"Dad!" Hailey called out, interrupting them. "Tyler's eating the dirt!"

"Well," Cassie said, moving on her crutches toward the door, "enough chitter chatter. Let's get to work."

Two days later, Cassie watched Devin haul an old mattress out of the director's cabin and heft it into the back of his pickup truck. His old, rusty pickup truck.

When she'd asked him how old it was, he'd just smirked and said it was paid off, so what did it matter? But she shuddered to think of him driving Hailey around in there—it looked like it was about two miles away from sputtering to a slow and painful death on the side of the road.

After he cleared out the cabin, he was going to sweep, then mop, then head to Home Depot to pick up a few buckets of mold control spray. Cassie had offered to clean the bathroom, but he'd insisted that she stay outside and watch the kids.

So here she was, lounging around with Hailey and Tyler, while Devin got things done.

Lots of things.

Lots of *physical* things that showed off his…rather impressive strength.

Yikes! Her face flamed. What was wrong with her? She didn't even like the guy! He was only here because she literally couldn't do any of this manual labor herself.

And even if she *did* like him, he was her little brother's buddy. She'd known him since he was five. The fact that she was noticing his muscles made her feel—ugh. It just felt wrong.

Three years' age difference is not *a big deal at this point in our lives.*

But that was hardly the point. Devin might be nice to look at, and he might be doing a good job clearing out the cabin, but she'd never trust him. Not with his history.

She had to admit that, so far, he was exceeding her expectations. Jared would have laughed in her face if she'd ever suggested he sweep, mop or apply mold control spray to anything.

Cassie shook her head. She still wasn't sure why she'd been so surprised when he'd asked her for a divorce. Over the years, he'd proven to her, time and again, that what mattered most to him was himself.

"Miss Cassie?" Hailey interrupted her walk down memory lane. "Can you do French braids?"

Cassie smiled at the girl. "It's been a while, but I'm sure it'll come back to me."

"Ooh!" Hailey flipped around so that Cassie could access her hair. "Can you do it now? I've wanted them *forever*, but Daddy's tried and tried, and he can't do it."

Cassie glanced over at Tyler, who was napping in his car seat in the shade of a tree, a winter cap on his head and a blanket draped over his little sleeping form. It was a clear day—sunny, but with a little bite. Winter's last gasp before spring rolled all the way in. Tyler was down to two naps a day, and both were generally between an hour and an hour and a half, for which Cassie was grateful. Although teething was ruining his nighttime sleep, so far, it hadn't interfered with his daytime rest.

Hailey had kept him entertained for quite a while before he conked out. She'd gotten down on her hands and knees, encouraging him to crawl. Tyler could rock back and forth on all fours, but he had yet to actually move. Which was more than okay with Cassie. If he started crawling now, while she was on crutches, it would be a disaster.

It had been cute to see how hard he laughed when Hailey was playing with him, though. Her little man. The baby she'd prayed for so many times over the years.

"Of course, honey. Scoot back a little," she said, gathering the girl's wavy hair into her hands. "Do you have a brush or a comb in your truck? This'll be easier if I get the knots out first."

Hailey shook her head. "My brush is at home in the bathroom. Why would we have it in the truck?"

Cassie smiled again. Why, indeed? "Do you mind if I brush it with my fingers? I'll be gentle."

"Sure!"

Cassie got to work. Hailey's hair was fine, but very tangled. "Does your dad help you brush your hair?"

"Sometimes."

"Do you brush it, too?"

"Yep, before school."

"What about before bed?"

"Why would I brush it before bed? Nobody's going to see me in the nighttime!"

"That's true," Cassie said, "but do you brush your *teeth* before bed?"

"A course!"

"How come? Nobody's going to see your teeth in the night, either."

Hailey paused for a long moment, crinkling her nose as she thought about it. "Because if I don't brush, I'll get cavities and my teeth will get brown and yucky and fall out!"

"You're right. And do you know what that's called? Preventative care. Because when you do it, you help *prevent* problems from developing in the future. You can do the same thing with your hair, too. Brushing it at night will make it easier to brush in the morning."

"Really?"

"Mm-hmm."

"Daddy never told me that."

"Well, your dad has short hair. He might not know that girls should brush their hair before bed as well as in the morning."

"I'll tell him!"

"Good idea."

Cassie got out as many of the knots as she could, then started weaving strands of the girl's hair together. "Okay." She twisted an elastic around the bottom of the braid. "All set."

"Ooh!" Hailey leaped to her feet, reaching up to feel the back of her head. "Can I see?"

"I don't have a mirror, but you can run inside the cabin really quick and take a peek in the bathroom."

Hailey took off at a trot.

A few minutes later, she came running back out of the cabin, towing her dad behind her. "Miss Cassie!" she gushed. "I love it sooooooo much!"

Cassie smiled. "I'm glad, honey." At least she'd been able to be of some small use despite her injury, even if she couldn't clean the cabin.

"Daddy! Can I call Avery on your phone and show her my French braid? She won't believe it!"

Devin sighed and took his phone out of his pocket. "Five minutes, peanut."

The little girl beamed as she snatched it out of his hand. "Thank you, thank you, thank you!" She ran off, already dialing her friend.

Devin shot Cassie an amused glance. "Are all little girls this chatty?"

Cassie chuckled. "Pretty much."

"The braid looks nice. She's wanted one of those for the longest time, and no matter how hard I tried, I just kept butchering it."

Cassie could imagine, and the mental picture of his haplessness with Hailey's hair made her smile transform into a full-out grin. "Happy to help."

"She told me you said she should brush her hair at night."

"It'll keep it less tangled."

"She also said I'm just a boy, so I wouldn't understand."

Cassie smothered a laugh. "I didn't phrase it quite like that…"

"Sure, you didn't," he said, winking. "Seriously, though. Thanks. There are some moments when I really wish her mother were more involved, but you just took a bit of that pressure off. I'm grateful."

"Is her mother local?"

He shook his head. "Not even close. But she might be moving back to Boston from Colorado this summer. We'll see."

"That would be good, wouldn't it?"

"Jury's out on that one, but we can hope."

"Why's the jury out? What's her deal?"

He sighed, pursing his lips as he turned his face up to the sky. "She's flaky. She says she'll do things, and then she doesn't. It upsets Hailey. But it's her mom, so we have to keep trying."

"Do you share custody?" Cassie knew she was being nosy, but she couldn't help it. She wanted to understand how he'd come to be a single dad.

"No. We never have. It's always just been me."

"That's unusual, isn't it?"

"Yeah, maybe. But she didn't even want to go through with the pregnancy, so I always knew what I was signing up for."

"Were the two of you married or…?"

"We were. Briefly. It was a stupid Vegas thing. Went for the weekend because our friends were eloping, and then we drank too much and decided *hey, wouldn't it be a great idea if we got married, too?* Her father had it annulled within a week. But surprise! Hailey didn't get the memo that the marriage was invalid."

"Wow. That's tough."

Devin shrugged. "Yes and no. It was a shock at the time, but ultimately it's the best thing that's ever happened to me, so I can't complain."

"Why didn't your ex want to go through with the pregnancy?" It was hard for Cassie to understand, given how long—and how fervently—she'd prayed for a baby. But she had nothing but respect for women who carried a pregnancy to term knowing that they couldn't, for whatever reason, raise the child. After all, that's what Tyler's biological mother had done.

Devin lifted an eyebrow, clearly unenthused about continuing the conversation. "Do you really want to get into this whole sad story right now?"

"Umm, yes? But if I'm being too nosy for you, you can tell me to knock it off."

He laughed. "All right, then, boss. Knock it off."

She held up her hands in surrender, then mimed zipping her lips. "Got it. None of my business. But if you ever need help with anything mom-related, like French braids or princess parties, just know that I'm always happy to help."

He stared at her for a second, his gray eyes intense. Not stormy, but steady. Solid. Secure. Her heart flip-flopped in her chest as warning bells went off in her head. *Trouble!*

"Her birthday's coming up in a few weeks," he said, "so I might just take you up on that."

Cassie swallowed hard. She'd made the offer flippantly, but suddenly, it felt anything but.

Chapter Three

The cabins were coming along. Devin had spent several weeks emptying them out, cleaning them up and repairing their roofs, porches and windows.

Cassie had helped a little with the cleaning, mostly while Hailey was at school and Tyler was either napping or content to hang out in his car seat. Devin didn't mind that he'd done the lion's share of the work. It had been nice to have some help with Hailey, and to have company.

Not that they'd had any deep conversations. Nope, after he'd revealed as much as he had about Shannon, Devin had kept a tight lid on anything even remotely personal. Given how unenthusiastic Cassie had been about him joining the team, he didn't want to give her any additional ammunition to make a case against keeping him on the payroll after she was back on her feet.

Tyler's front teeth had finally come in, so he'd been pretty content, all things considered. Devin didn't even mind the fact that he had to stop whatever he was working on every once in a while to pick Tyler up and move him to wherever Cassie needed him to be.

He liked it, actually. Babies were fun, and since he'd already gone through the baby stage with Hailey, he had more confidence with Tyler than he'd had back then.

He'd been so nervous with Hailey at first. She'd been so tiny and had seemed so breakable. It had been almost inconceivable to him that the doctor had actually let him take his daughter home. Who was he to be entrusted with complete responsibility for another human being? And a helpless one, at that.

"You'll get the hang of it," one of the nurses had said to him, squeezing his shoulder, and he had. But it hadn't been easy, and it hadn't been quick. He still felt like he was failing Hailey a lot of the time.

The stakes were lower with Tyler, since he wasn't Devin's kid. Plus, he was cute. Chubby. Happy. Smiley. Devin knew Cassie wanted to adopt him, and he hoped it worked out for her. She was a great mom.

"So." Cassie was perched on the edge of a bottom bunk in one of the camper cabins. They'd just put in new mattresses yesterday, and he was currently installing the vinyl mattress covers that were both waterproof and bugproof on all sixteen of the twin bunk beds. "When do you think we can move in?"

Devin paused and glanced around the camper cabin. Once he finished with these mattress covers, this cabin would be all set. He'd finish the other camper cabins today, and tomorrow, he'd start cleaning out the dining hall. The director's and nurse's cabins were already complete.

"They're done," he said, "so whenever you want."

"When are you moving?"

"Next weekend, when my lease is up." It was still hard to believe that he wouldn't have to pay rent. He just had to hope that everything they were doing to get the camp ready to reopen would pay off, and this would be a job he could keep for years to come.

She nodded. "I want to move in now, but I can't leave Aunt Mirriam's until my knee is better. I have to wait until I'm off the crutches and can lift Tyler out of his crib."

"How's the physical therapy going?" She'd been going to

appointments in Wychmere Bay three mornings a week since the accident.

"It's fine."

"How much longer do they think you'll be on crutches?"

"Another week or two."

"Oh, well that's nothing."

She narrowed her eyes, picked up a crutch and pointed it at him. "Easy for you to say."

He chuckled, holding up his hands in mock surrender. "True."

"Will you help me pack in the meantime? I know it's not part of your job description, but it would really help me out."

"Helping you *is* part of my job description."

She gave her head a stubborn shake. "Only with Tyler, and only when we're here at camp."

He rolled his eyes. "Yes, boss, I'll help you pack."

She rolled her eyes right back. "When are you going to knock it off with all this boss nonsense?"

"Hmm." He pretended to think about it. "Maybe when you're no longer my boss."

"You know we don't have a hierarchy here."

"Well," he said, lips twitching, "that may be true, but I was always taught to respect my elders."

Immediately, from the look on her face, Devin could tell that he'd pushed it too far. He really needed to learn to think before he spoke. "Sorry, Cass. I'm just kidding."

"It's true, though. I'm older than you."

"Barely." He was twenty-seven, and if he remembered correctly from when they were kids, her thirtieth birthday would have taken place back at the end of January. Three years had been a big gap when they were in school, but not so much anymore.

Or he wanted to believe it wasn't, anyway.

Stop fooling yourself into imagining you could have a shot with her.

She looked away, obviously not convinced that he didn't think she was ancient, and he wanted to kick himself. *Way to make her uncomfortable, genius.* "Of course I'll help you pack. It would be pretty uncharitable of me to say no after everything you've been doing for Hailey."

She waved that off. "I love doing things with Hailey."

"And she loves doing things with you." French braids, friendship bracelets, painting seashells, painting their nails… all sorts of girly things he didn't have the time or inclination to do.

The fact that they'd be next door neighbors here at Camp Piper wasn't lost on him, either. Seeing how much Hailey looked up to Cassie made Shannon's absence even more stark. He was hopeful that the close proximity meant Cassie would continue to be a friend, mentor and role model to his little girl.

As long as he didn't do anything to mess it up.

"How's summer registration going, by the way?" Alex had created a website for the camp, and they'd officially launched the registration page last week.

Cassie grimaced. "Umm…slow."

"How slow?"

"Slow, slow. So far the only people who've visited the registration page are…us."

Devin's eyes bugged with both disbelief and concern. "Nobody but us has visited the page? Not even one person?"

"We'll get the word out. Alex is working on putting together social media pages for us as we speak."

"Social media doesn't do much for a local business like this. The country club's social media got *maybe* two likes a post, but that place was always crowded. Offline is always better than online. We need to mail out flyers, put up posters and start making presentations at schools and after-school clubs, stuff like that."

She chewed her lip. "I think we need to figure out more about what we're going to be offering before we go all-in on the promotion. How can we walk into a school and tell them about how awesome Camp Piper is when we don't even know how we're going to structure a day?"

"Okay, then we need to get cracking on that. Like, yesterday."

"I know. But we need to get the dining hall ready, too."

"Let me worry about that. You call your brothers and get them out here on the weekend. We can take a look at the equipment in the storage shed and see what's still viable."

"Good idea," she said, already pulling out her phone.

"Should we invite your aunt, too?"

Cassie shook her head. "She doesn't want to be involved with the day-to-day operations."

That was wild to him, that she'd be willing to bankroll the camp without being involved, but who was he to question Miriam's business decisions?

He was just grateful for the job. His parents hadn't had much money when he was growing up, and he'd never had much money, either. Dropping out of college and taking an hourly job as a lifeguard to support your newborn baby would do that to you.

Over the years, there had been a few people who'd urged him to hire a lawyer so he could get child support payments from Shannon. He'd never wanted to go through with it, though, for a couple of reasons. First, when she'd agreed not to terminate the pregnancy, he'd promised he'd never ask her for anything, and he was determined to keep his word. Second, he worried that if he ever *did* ask her for financial assistance, she'd return the favor by pursuing custody.

He couldn't risk it.

Just like he couldn't risk losing this job now—either because the camp failed to launch, or because his big mouth made Cassie kick him to the curb.

Cassie stared at the mess of equipment strewn around the shed. Tangled-up fishing rods, torn soccer nets, peeling volleyballs, discolored kayaks, split arrows, rusty hatchets, broken boogie boards…she hardly knew where to look.

"Well, this isn't great," Jonah said, hands on his hips and a frown on his face.

"Nope," Alex agreed. Her youngest brother was using his cane today, not his forearm crutches. Prior to hurting her knee, Cassie had never had to use crutches before, and her sympathy for her brother—who'd been using mobility aids his entire life—had shot through the roof.

He'd hate that, of course. The effects of cerebral palsy were something he dealt with on a daily basis, but the disorder didn't define him, and he didn't like it when people focused on it.

"Should we pull it all out?" Devin asked. "Sort through it?"

"Let's do it," Jonah said, and the two of them started hauling everything out onto the grass.

Although Cassie was wearing a sweater, Devin and her brothers were all in short sleeves. Spring on Cape Cod was pleasant, but unpredictable. Temperatures could be in the forties or the seventies. It was sunnier than the winter months, but still overcast about half the time. Last year, a nor'easter had even brought snow in May!

Alex took a step back. "Wanna walk down to the marsh while they do their thing?"

Cassie glanced in the direction of the ocean. It was a bit of a hike, but beyond the marsh, the water was calm and sparkly. "Sure."

They headed down the path leading to the wooden boardwalk that overlooked the marsh, a maze of tiny tide pools and creeks amidst the tall sea grass. Alex was usually the slowest of the group, and she could tell that he was enjoying having to slow down so she could catch up. "Where's the baby?"

"Aunt Mirriam took him to a playgroup at that baby gym in Wychmere Bay. The one the pastor's wife owns."

"Oh, that's cool." They both attended Wychmere Community Church and knew Amanda Kobayashi-Anderson.

They stopped and leaned on the boardwalk railing, looking down into the marsh. This would be a great spot for fishing, right here off the boardwalk. And if they waded into the water, it would also be an excellent place to dig for clams.

"Do you think we're crazy," she asked, "trying to open the camp so quickly?"

Her brother's lips quirked up, his eyes a shade of blue that was similar to the sky. "Oh, definitely. Certifiable."

She swatted at his arm. "Seriously? You don't think we can do it?"

"Hey now." He batted her hand away. "I didn't say that."

"I'll be honest with you. I didn't think we were going to get the cabins done so quickly."

"Devin's not just a baby whisperer—he's a workhorse."

"Yeah," she agreed, thinking about how dedicated he was to getting things done both quickly and correctly, "he kind of is."

A couple of wispy clouds skittered across the sun, casting shadows, while a flock of seagulls flew by. Their breeding season had begun, so they were especially loud these days.

Alex rested his hip against the wooden railing. "It's not often I get to say I told you so to my big sis, but… I told you so."

"Yeah, yeah. Spare me the gloating, squirt."

He laughed. "I'm half a foot taller than you!"

She patted his cheek in a lofty and over-the-top manner. "But you'll always be my baby bro."

"For what it's worth," he said seriously, "I've never seen him drink."

"Good thing you didn't tag along with Jonah back when he was in high school." There was a three-year age gap between Cassie and Jonah, and a four-year gap between Jonah and Alex.

"Yeah," he said sarcastically, "good thing." He'd had a hard time finding his social footing in school, while Jonah had been Mr. Popular. Cassie, for her part, had fallen somewhere in between. Not the most popular girl in school, but not a pariah, either.

"Be grateful. You didn't need any of that drama. And look at you now."

"Yup, head of accounting at a nursing home." He pointed his thumbs at his face. "Life of the party right here."

Her brother and his self-deprecating sense of humor drove her nuts sometimes. He didn't work at a nursing home—he worked at one of those fifty-five-plus retirement communities where the residents were always out living their best lives on the tennis court, the golf course and the beach.

"If I had any friends your age, you know I'd be sending them your way."

Alex's face froze in horror. "Don't you dare."

Cassie bit back a laugh. "*If*, little brother. I said *if*."

"I hate setups," he grumbled.

"How else are you going to meet anybody?"

"How do *you* meet people these days?"

She fluttered her hand in surprise. After everything Jared had put her through, did he seriously think she'd be interested in *dating*?

But then again, she'd never told her family the full story of why they'd split. At first, when she was still married, she'd hidden the truth to protect her family's relationship with Jared. And then, after he'd filed for divorce, she'd simply been too ashamed.

Although she'd done nothing wrong, she'd been the one to pay the price, while he'd moved on as though none of it had ever happened.

If she let it, the whole situation could still make her terribly, irredeemably sad. She could only hope that one day, with God's help, she'd be able to fully let it go and move on.

"Oh, I'm done with all that. I've got Tyler now. I'm good."

"Maybe I'm done with all that, too."

"Done? You haven't even started." Although her brother had dated a little, he'd never had a real relationship. And he had so much to offer! But if he wasn't ready, she knew she shouldn't push.

"You want to hassle someone about dating, hassle Jonah. I don't have time for all that noise. Especially not now, while we're trying to get this camp back on its feet."

She sighed, wishing her knee would hurry up and heal so she could actually contribute something meaningful to the cause.

Alex turned back to the ocean. "You're good with him now, though, right? Devin? You're not holding it over his head?"

She wrinkled her nose. "Do I seem like a vengeful person to you?"

"You weren't exactly shy about letting us all know that you were against us bringing him on board."

"Tyler was teething, I hadn't slept in what felt like a million years and then Aunt Mirriam blindsided all of us with that. How was I the only one of us who was upset?"

Alex shrugged. "I've always liked Devin."

"Because you never saw what an immature idiot he was."

Alex arched an eyebrow. "When he was a teenager? Aren't we all immature idiots at that age?"

"Speak for yourself, young 'un. I was neither immature nor an idiot."

“No, I guess not. You were like a little adult even when we were kids.”

Cassie blinked. Was that supposed to be a compliment? Because all it did was remind her of the arguments she’d had with Jared near the end of their marriage, when he would come home drunk and try to start drama: *Get mad at me! Tell me you hate me! I deserve it!*

And when she’d refuse to engage, he’d get mean: *Responsible Cassie. Reliable Cassie. Washed-up, boring, infertile Cassie.*

She backed away from those memories lickety-split.

Alex flicked a glance toward camp. “Think we should head back, see if they’ve made any headway?”

“Sure.”

“And for the record,” he said, “I think we’re just crazy enough to pull this off. But we’ve got to put our heads down and do the work. All four of us. And *you* need to get over whatever your hangup is with Devin.”

“I’m over it, Alex. Devin and I are good.” The breeze kicked up, ruffling her hair, and she shivered, pulling her sweater tighter around her chest.

“Does *he* know that?”

“Of course he does.”

“Could’ve fooled me.”

“What do you mean?”

He shrugged. “There’s a vibe between you two. Like he’s walking on eggshells.”

“That’s ridiculous.” Wasn’t it?

It had been weeks now that they’d been working together, and although it was sometimes awkward, overall it was fine, right? Especially with the kids as a buffer.

Maybe today, while they were both kid-less, she should clear the air.

She might have been opposed to working with him at first, but she wasn't anymore. He'd more than proven his worth.

If he was still walking on eggshells, she needed to let him know he should stop. His job was safe—at least from her perspective.

The overall success of Camp Piper, however, was still up in the air.

Chapter Four

Devin was hosing off the sea kayaks while Cassie took Alex and Jonah to go look at the area he'd cleared for woodcraft, where the campers would learn to chop wood, build fires and practice wilderness first aid. The kayaks were faded but structurally intact, so that was a relief. The fishing rods, however, were a mess, as was the archery equipment. They'd have to decide if they wanted to restock those items or figure out other activities to fill in the gaps.

The good news was that the camp had a basketball court and space to play both soccer and volleyball, all of which would only require them to buy a few new nets and balls. So sports would for sure be one of the activity blocks campers could choose from.

Swimming was another green light, since they had the pond. They'd also been given the go-ahead from the town to rope off a small section of the water at Piper Beach just for the campers, where they could use boogie boards and snorkeling equipment and generally splash around in the ocean. Devin would have to hire some lifeguards and swim instructors, but that would be easy—he had plenty of experience hiring for those jobs.

The Reeds all wanted to keep the camp schedule similar to what it had been when they were little: wake up at seven, breakfast at eight, one-hour activity blocks from nine until noon, followed by an hour for lunch, an hour-long "rest period" in the cabins, then three more one-hour activity blocks until dinner. After dinner, there would be special activities like bonfires, movie nights and camp-wide scavenger hunts.

Between swimming, arts and crafts, kayaking, shore ecology, hiking, sports and woodcraft, they had seven daily activity periods covered. Ideally, they'd have at least ten activities to choose from so the kids could have some variety over the course of their stay.

He finished spraying down the last kayak and shut off the hose.

"How's it going?" Cassie called out, coming up the path on her crutches. She had color in her cheeks, and her hair was windblown. He wished he wasn't quite so aware of how attractive she was; it made working together complicated, and he'd had enough complications with Shannon to last a lifetime.

He hauled one of the boats back into the shed. "They were dirty—lots of dust and cobwebs—but they're not damaged."

"Phew. Kayaks are expensive."

"True." He picked up another one. It was still wet, and it soaked through his jeans, making him shiver. He was done with this wacky, up-and-down springtime weather: bring on the summertime heat! "Anything else we should be doing while Alex and Jonah are here?"

"They actually just left."

"Oh."

"But I wanted to talk to you about something."

"Sure," he said, feeling wary. He hoped the three of them hadn't conferred and decided that he and Hailey shouldn't move onsite after all. He knew it was hasty, moving here before his trial period officially ended, but the savings were enough to offset the risk. "Let me just put this last kayak inside."

He deposited the boat on the rack inside the shed, wiped his hands on his pants and came back out. "What's up?"

"I told Jonah and Alex what you said about putting up flyers and speaking to schools, and they liked the idea."

"Great."

"Jonah suggested doing an open house, too. We can put it on the flyers and get people out here to experience what camp's like for themselves."

"That's perfect. How could anyone not fall in love with the place once they see it?"

"Exactly." She smiled, and he felt like a dopey teenager again, basking in it.

"Did you guys discuss a date?"

"Do you think a month gives us enough time to finish getting things up and running?"

"I don't see why not. The dining hall's big, but it won't take that long. After that, all that's left is putting in the security cameras and getting the activities set up." Why the camp needed security cameras was beyond him, but Mirriam was insisting.

Cassie nodded, the sun showing off glints of green and gold in her hazel eyes. "Does Mother's Day weekend seem doable to you?"

"The Saturday? Or Mother's Day itself?"

"The Saturday."

"It's doable. School gets out at the end of June, so parents will definitely be thinking about their summer plans by then. And I don't think that's a big travel weekend, so it should be fine."

"Yeah, we didn't think Memorial Day weekend would work, since the locals go out of town and the tourists who're here that weekend most likely won't be around during the summer, anyway."

"Right."

"What do you think about doing it in the afternoon and inviting people to stay for a cookout at the campfires?"

"That could be fun."

"We could even host a dance in the dining room, turn it into a big event for the community. My aunt and uncle used to hold a big dance at the end of the summer, but I think a kick-off on the day of the open house would be a good draw for getting people out to see what Camp Piper's all about."

"Like a family dance?"

She nodded.

"That's a great idea." Hailey and all her little friends loved the family dances at school. It would definitely attract the elementary school crowd.

"Okay, I'll tell Alex and Jonah and start working on the flyers."

"Perfect," he said, thinking that was the end of the conversation. Apparently it wasn't, though, because Cassie didn't move. "I should go get Hailey, unless there was something else you wanted to talk about?"

"Umm…" Her face heated. "Actually there is."

"What's up?"

"Well, uh…" She scratched at the ground with one of her crutches. "Alex said something that got me thinking…"

"O-kay…" He had no idea where she was going with this.

"Do I make you nervous?"

Not what he'd expected her to say. And not a question he wanted to answer. "Uh…in what way?"

"Alex said it seems like you're walking on eggshells around me."

Devin felt his shoulders relax a fraction of an inch. She wasn't asking if he was attracted to her. Thank goodness. "This job's important to me."

"It's important to me, too."

He shook his head. She didn't get it. "You're a nurse, Cassie. You can always get a new job."

"You could get a new job, too."

"Nurses make about three times what lifeguards make, and your job's available year round."

She scrunched her brow. "But you weren't just a lifeguard. You ran the whole aquatics program at the country club."

"For the last two years, I did. But how many of those jobs do you think there are around here? And how many of the places that have that job available are hiring right now? I'll give you an idea." He made a circle with his right hand, held it up to his eye and looked at her through the center. "Zero."

"Really? There's no one who's hiring?"

"Not on Cape Cod. I could maybe catch an interview or two up in Boston, but the cost of living there is bonkers, and I don't want to uproot Hailey from her school. If I applied at the YMCA in Wychmere Bay, they'd probably have a spot for a swim instructor or a lifeguard, but I'd have to take a big pay cut. And they might not need me after the summer's over. It's a very seasonal industry."

"What made you choose that line of work?"

"I dropped out of college when Hailey was born. Swimming was the only marketable skill I had."

Cassie frowned. "That can't be true."

"Oh, it's true. I wasn't exactly the best or the brightest student." Before he dropped out, he'd been on the six-year graduation plan, much to his parents' chagrin. "It was either swim, wait tables or give car sales a shot."

The ghost of a smile flickered across her face. "I've heard those guys make bank."

"Car salesmen? Sure, some of them. But most of them crash and burn within a few months. The turnover rate at car dealerships is something like sixty-seven percent a year."

Cassie's eyes popped. "Whoa. And I thought the turnover rate for nurses was high."

"What is it for nursing?"

"Around eighteen percent."

"So car sales seemed like a dicey proposition. Plus, I didn't have anyone to watch Hailey. At the country club, employees got to use the childcare center for free."

"That's a good perk."

"Yeah, when I got fired, I was *stressing*. But then your aunt came along and dangled this opportunity in front of me. And I get it that we don't have the best history, and that your distrust is essentially all my own fault, so yeah. I get nervous sometimes. Especially after I put my foot in my mouth. I don't want you to wake up after you're out of that brace and convince everyone that you guys really don't need me after all."

Cassie's face fell. "You think I'd fire you after my knee recovers?"

He lifted his shoulder. "I don't know, Cass. But I'm not willing to take that chance."

"I'm not going to fire you, Devin. I wouldn't do that to you. Or Hailey."

He took a deep breath, studying her for a second. "I'm sorry I was such an idiot in high school. I'm sorry you had to see me like that."

"Can I ask, are you in a program?"

"Like AA?"

She nodded.

"I went to AA meetings at the beginning, and they helped, but I like Celebrate Recovery better. It's Bible-based, and you can go for all kinds of different reasons—alcoholism, anger, codependency, food issues, whatever. It's nice to have a group of guys I can talk to about what's going on in my life at any given moment."

"I've heard of Celebrate Recovery."

"Yeah, they have it every Friday night at my church in Wychmere Bay."

"Wait. Which church?"

"Wychmere Community Church—you've probably seen it on your way back and forth to the highway."

"Uh, I've been a lot closer than that. That's where I go, too."

He rubbed his jaw, his hand scraping across his five-o'clock shadow. "No way. Which service?"

"Sundays at nine."

"Ah, okay. Hailey and I go at eleven so she can go to Sunday school."

A flock of seagulls made a big commotion as they flew overhead, and Cassie glanced up to take them in. "I can't believe you go to WCC."

"Small world, isn't it?"

"What time do you have to pick up Hailey?"

He pulled out his phone and checked the time. "Soon."

"Would you mind dropping me off at Aunt Mirriam's?" With her injury, driving was not advised. "I can call Alex to come back if it's too much trouble."

"No trouble." Provided his truck started. He'd replaced the battery a few days ago, but the ignition was already having problems turning over again—one of the many joys of driving a beater. "Just let me put the hose away." He shook out the last of the water droplets, then looped it into a coil and hung it on the holder on the side of the shed. "Ready?"

She nodded, and they started up the path back to the parking lot. "What are you doing for dinner?" she asked, after he helped her step up and slide into the passenger seat, then maneuver her crutches onto her lap.

He closed the door for her, then came around to his side. "I don't know. Mac and cheese, probably."

"You should come over to Aunt Mirriam's. I put chili in the slow cooker this morning. We've got a ton."

"Meh," he said, adjusting the rearview mirror, then turning on the truck with—thankfully—no problems at all, "we wouldn't want to put you out."

"You'd be *helping* us. Two people won't even make a dent in the mountain of chili I've got cooking."

He gave her a sideways look. "Are you sure?"

"Super sure."

"All right, then. Thanks. I like chili." He also liked the fact that he'd laid his fear about losing his job at her feet, and she hadn't kicked him in the face.

If he didn't have to worry about getting fired, then all he needed to worry about was making sure the camp was a success.

He prayed those wouldn't be famous last words.

"Argh!" Hailey squealed, spitting her chili back into her bowl and fanning her face with her hands.

Cassie's eyes went wide with horror. What had just happened? This was very mild chili, with only a touch of chili pepper and cayenne. There were no jalapenos or habaneros in the recipe—just a few sweet bell peppers, along with beans, carrots, zucchini, corn and crushed tomatoes.

Devin snickered and pushed Hailey's cup of milk closer to her. "Okay, drama queen. We get it. You don't like veggies."

The little girl pouted. "They're yucky, Daddy."

"But Miss Cassie went to a lot of trouble to make you this nice meal."

"Oh, no—it's fine," Cassie protested. "She doesn't have to eat it if she doesn't want to."

"Do you want some pasta instead, honey?" Aunt Mirriam asked. "We have leftover spaghetti in the fridge."

"Ooh!" Hailey perked right up. "I love psghetti!"

Devin sighed. "Pasta sauce counts as a vegetable, right?"

"Sorry to be the one to break it to you but…tomatoes are a fruit," Cassie said, winking at Hailey.

"So are cucumbers, Daddy! We learned it in school!"

"Argh! No!" He dropped his head to his hands, giving Cassie a pretty big clue about where Hailey's penchant for drama came from. "I'm failing as a father, then, because you don't eat any real vegetables at all!"

Hailey giggled, and Tyler, from his high chair, gave a little giggle-squeal and banged his hands on his tray.

Aunt Mirriam got up to heat up a bowl of spaghetti, and Cassie gave Tyler another rice cracker, which he grabbed with both hands and shoved straight into his mouth.

"Miss Cassie," Hailey said, once her steaming plate of spaghetti was in front of her, "it's gonna be my birthday soon!"

"Your dad mentioned that to me. How old are you turning?"

"Seven!"

"Wow, seven! You're getting so old! You're going to be a grandma before you know it!"

The little girl dissolved into a fit of laughter.

"Tell her what you want to do for your party, peanut," Devin prompted.

"I want to have a tea party!"

Cassie shot a quick glance at Devin, who nodded, like *yeah, she's for real, but I have no idea how to put a tea party together.* "That sounds fun," she said. "Where do you want to have it?" Maybe she could do a little recon for him.

"There's this place…it's so nice…it's called, um… I don't remember, but it's nice and cute and fun! I want to go there!"

"Have you been there before?"

"Yes!"

"When?"

"Jenny's birthday party!"

Devin's eyes lit up in recognition. "That party was at Captain Cod's Olde English Inn."

"Captain Cod!" Hailey repeated. "That's so funny!"

"That *is* a funny name," Cassie agreed. "I don't think fish can be ship captains, can they?"

"Fish can't go on ships," the little girl informed her, "or else they couldn't breathe!"

"You're right. Do you think fish drown in the air the way people drown in water?"

"Mmm." Hailey scrunched her brow in confusion. "Maybe. But you should take swimming lessons with me, Miss Cassie. Then you wouldn't drown."

Cassie chuckled. "Thanks, sweetheart, but it's okay. I can swim. That was a hypothetical question."

"A hypo-*what*-ical question?"

Cassie waved her hand. "Don't worry about it. I was just trying to be silly."

"Will you come to my birthday party?"

"Oh! Well, I'd like to, but you and your dad should probably talk about your guest list before you start inviting people."

"Daddy." Hailey sat up straight in her chair, only the little bit of tomato sauce on her chin marring her sudden foray into seriousness. "Can Miss Cassie please come to my party?"

"We'll talk about that later, peanut."

"But Daddy—"

"Later, Hailey. We need to figure out the time and place before we throw invitations out there. And right now, it's time to focus on eating your dinner."

"Humph," she grumbled, but then she picked up her fork and twirled her spaghetti.

"Hoo-waaa!" Tyler squealed, slapping his hands onto his high-chair tray.

Hailey perked back up. "He's babbling! He's babbling!"

"He sure is," Cassie said, scooping her last bite of chili into her mouth before asking the baby, "Are you still hungry?" Before she'd hurt her knee, she'd gotten used to multitasking at mealtimes. Staying with Aunt Mirriam had given her a break from that, but she'd have to get back into the swing of things before too long. Cassie had her fingers crossed that she'd be off the crutches and back on her feet by this time next week.

"Should I get him the pears?" Aunt Mirriam asked, getting up from her seat.

"I can do it," Cassie said.

"Pfft. Don't you dare. I'm done eating anyway. And I think little Miss Hailey Boo will help me feed him, won't you, darlin'?"

"Yes!" she cried, clapping her hands.

"You two head on into the living room," Aunt Mirriam said, shooing Cassie and Devin out with a flick of her wrist. "Devin, you can grab that plate of cookies on the counter and take them with you. I made two different kinds: Cape Cod molasses and cranberry pecan."

Devin picked up the cookies while Cassie crutched her way into the living room.

"So," she said, sitting down on the couch, "a tea party at Captain Cod's Olde English Inn, huh?"

Devin's gray eyes sparkled. "Good old Captain Cod. Hope he doesn't drown in the air before the party."

Cassie laughed. "Stop. I know it was a dumb thing to say."

"It wasn't dumb." He grinned. "It was hilarious."

"Well, then, you're welcome. Always happy to provide the comic relief."

Devin picked up a molasses cookie and then sat back in his seat. "You're going to help me throw this party, right?"

"Oh, I am, am I?"

"You have to. I can't organize a tea party on my own."

"Didn't you go to that other little girl's party?"

"Sure, but I was the only dad there. I didn't really participate."

"Why not?" Cassie picked up her own cookie—the cranberry pecan cookies were her favorite of the two. She especially loved Aunt Mirriam's delicious orange glaze. Soft, sweet and so, so good.

"I don't know, Cass, it's awkward. All those fussy little sandwiches? Plus, all those moms know each other, and they gossip. I'm not into that."

"They gossip in front of the kids?"

He shook his head. "The kids were at one table, the moms were at another. Hailey didn't need me lurking there, so I went into the lobby and checked sports stats on my phone." What was it with men and sports? He and Jonah were cut from the exact same cloth.

"Okay, then it doesn't sound like it'll be that hard to organize. The venue will do most of the work."

"I really can't afford to book a party at Captain Cod's, though. I looked it up just now. Even the cheapest option is thirty-five dollars a person. I'm going to need to bootstrap it."

"You can do it at the camp! When's her birthday?"

"Two weeks."

"That's perfect, then. We can do it in the dining hall." It would actually be a good trial run—on a much smaller scale—for the open house and family dance.

He gave her a hopeful look. "We…?"

She ignored it, because it was fun to give him a hard time. "What kind of entertainment did her little friend have?"

He grimaced. "Unicorns."

Cassie let out a startled laugh. "What?"

"There was a pony. With flowers. And a horn. The girls all got to ride it."

"At Captain Cod's Olde English Inn?"

Devin nodded. "In the back. On the beach. And then they made flower necklace thingies."

"Sounds like quite the party." She shook her head. Parents these days were *wild*. When she was a kid, her mom let the partygoers loose in the backyard for a couple of hours, then fed them pizza and cake before sending them back home. Now? It was all ponies and princesses and bounce house slides.

"But see? I can't just give them little sandwiches. Their expectations are high. I'm going to need to come up with something as cool as a unicorn."

Innocently batting her eyelashes, Cassie said, "But what could ever be as cool as a unicorn?"

Devin threw his hands in the air. "Nothing! See? That's the problem. And how on earth am I supposed to figure out what a bunch of seven-year-old girls are gonna like?"

"Okay, settle down there, friend. We'll figure it out."

His whole face slackened with relief. "You'll help?"

"It's for Hailey. Of course I'll help."

The little girl had already worked her way right into Cassie's heart.

And Devin? He was definitely still trouble, just not in the way she'd originally imagined he might be.

No, now her worry wasn't that he'd mess up the camp reopening for them. It was that he just might sneak past all her defenses and trick her into believing she could have another shot at romance.

Crooked smile aside, she'd have to stay strong and remember that no man would want to deal with the scars her ex had left when he'd walked out the door.

Chapter Five

Devin carted another box from the back of his pickup truck into the cabin and deposited it on the living room floor. Almost done. Then all he'd have to do was unpack.

He looked around the cabin in satisfaction. It wasn't as modern as his old apartment had been, but it was bigger. And whereas he and Hailey hadn't even had a backyard at their old place, now she could step outside and explore twenty-five acres of land. Plus, she could attend summer camp for free!

Provided he and the Reeds managed to get the camp open, that was. He still wasn't completely sure they were going to be able to pull it off.

"Knock, knock." Cassie peeked her head into the cabin from the open front door.

He wiped the sweat off his forehead with the back of his sleeve. "Come in."

Dressed casually in jeans and a Boston College sweatshirt, her hair pulled back into a ponytail, she walked in on her own two feet. "Hey! You're off the crutches!"

"Woot woot!" She grinned. "Got to keep wearing the brace for another week or two, but I've been cleared to pick up Tyler, so we can finally get out of Aunt Mirriam's hair."

"That's great. Where is the little rascal?"

"Napping in the portable crib Aunt Mirriam helped me set

up next door." She logged onto her phone and showed Devin a live feed of Tyler, sucking his thumb in his sleep.

"Aww, look at that. Does it alert you when he wakes up?"

"Yep, it's better than a traditional baby monitor, but Aunt Mirriam's over there with him, too. She wanted to come see the progress we've made." Cassie scanned the boxes scattered across the floor. "And look at you, getting settled. How much more stuff do you have?"

"One more box, and then I get to start unpacking."

"Want some help?"

"Sure." Devin nodded toward his kitchen counter. "There's a box cutter over there. Start anywhere you want."

Cassie grabbed it while he went back outside for the last box.

"Where do you want Hailey's clothes?" she called out as he came back in.

"The smaller bedroom. But I'll get it. You save your strength for Tyler."

"It's not that heavy," she protested.

"Still," he said, plucking the box out of her hands. "Your knee's not out of the woods yet."

She sighed and followed him into Hailey's room, which was the very definition of bare bones. "Where's her bedding?" she asked.

He waved his hand toward the living room. "In one of the boxes."

"Any idea which one? You didn't label them."

"No clue."

She shook her head. "Men."

"It's not like we have *that* many."

"I'll go investigate."

"Had any brilliant ideas for the party yet?" he called out as he transferred his daughter's clothes from the box into her dresser.

"Actually, yes." She came back to Hailey's room, propping her hip on the door, the box cutter still in hand.

"And…? Spill it."

A tiny smile danced at the corners of her mouth. "Mermaids."

"Mermaids?" he repeated skeptically.

"Mermaids." She gave a decisive nod. "They're the princesses of the sea."

"Okay," he said slowly, "so what are the mermaids going to do at the tea party?"

"That's the beauty of it! We can do so many things! We can do face painting, paint seashells, build sandcastles, blow bubbles, have a hula hoop contest… I can literally think of a dozen different activities we could do with them after the tea party part of the party."

Devin stroked his chin, unconvinced. "Who's going to do the face painting?"

"That's just a suggestion. But if you want to have face painting, I bet Amanda Anderson knows some people. They're always hosting birthday parties at the kids' gym in Wychmere Bay."

"And the other stuff? I can't afford anything expensive."

"Me! So that part won't cost you anything. I'll dress up and everything."

"As a mermaid? With a fish tail?" He was struggling to picture it.

She giggled, and it was about the prettiest sound he'd ever heard. "You're familiar with the Little Mermaid, right? She lives on land *and* in the sea."

His lips quirked up. "I don't know, boss. Without the tail, I think they're gonna feel cheated."

"*You* can always put on a tail."

He snorted. "A Merman? I don't think so."

"We could get you a trident to go with it. Those are *very* manly."

"Uh-huh." She was ridiculous, but it was low-key adorable to see her so excited about her ideas for the party.

Shannon hadn't even remembered Hailey's birthday last year, let alone offered to help host a party. If only…

Nope.

Devin cut that train of thought off at the knees. He couldn't wish he'd done things differently in the past, because then he wouldn't have Hailey.

But if he ever started dating again, if he ever got married for real, he'd look for a woman who showed up for the day-to-day, who found joy in the little things and who actually *wanted* to have a family.

"What else do they serve at a tea party besides the little sandwiches?" he asked.

"Macarons," she replied immediately and decisively.

"What are those?"

She gasped. "You've never had a macaron?"

"No. What is it? Some kind of macaroni?"

"No. No, no, no." She grabbed his arm and started pulling him toward the doorway.

"What are you doing?"

"We're going to get Tyler up from his nap so we can take you to the bakery for a macaron."

"Cassie!" He laughed, gently dislodging his arm from her grasp. "You never wake a sleeping baby."

"You do for emergencies."

"A macaron is not an emergency."

"It is when you've never had one! That's not just an emergency, it's—it's criminal!" she sputtered.

"What are they? Little cakes?"

"They're only the best cookies in the whole entire world, that's what."

"Definitely don't wake Tyler up for a cookie."

She slapped her hands on her hips. "These aren't just any cookies, buster. These are two light and airy meringue wafers with a layer of buttercream or jam in the middle. Cherry, blueberry, strawberry, pistachio, rose. The flavors are just..." She did a chef's kiss. "Honestly, they're a dream."

He worked hard to keep a straight face as he asked, "So they're sandwich cookies? Like Oreos? But fruit-flavored?"

She gave him a pained look. "Please tell me you're joking."

"I've never had one! I don't know what they're like."

Her phone alarm went off, and she glanced at the video of Tyler's crib. "Oh, he's awake. Come on. I'll check his diaper and then we'll go."

"You seriously want to head over to the bakery right now? I have to unpack. And what about Mirriam?"

She arched an eyebrow. "I'm doing you a favor by helping with the party, aren't I? Humor me on this. We can bring Aunt Mirriam with us, but now that we're talking about macarons, I have a craving."

So did Devin. But his had nothing to do with food—it was all about spending more time with her.

Sandpiper Sweets was one of Cassie's favorite places in town. Devin pulled into a metered parking spot a few doors down, and she got out of the car and unclipped Tyler from his seat. When she started to lift him out, Devin nudged her arm. "Let me get him," he said. "We don't want to overtax your knee." Aunt Mirriam had decided not to join them, so it was just the three of them for this outing.

Cassie stepped aside. Devin popped the baby onto his shoulder. "Hey, big guy."

"Blaaaaaa!" Tyler squawked in his ear, a happy grin on his chubby little face.

They passed the local coffee shop, Sea Beans, which was

packed with people sipping on signature drinks like the lavender blossom latte, mocha caramel breeze and banana boat latte. Next door, Lilly Shaughnessy's salon, The Lilly Pad, was bustling with ladies waiting for a cut, color or manicure.

"We should ask Lilly if we can put the flyer about the open house and family dance in her window," Devin suggested. "This is where all the moms at Hailey's school come to do their hair."

"Great idea. We'll ask Aurora at the bakery, too."

Cassie threw open the door to Sandpiper Sweets and inhaled deeply. The scents hit her all at once: vanilla, cinnamon, chocolate and freshly baked bread. The bright yellow walls, pink-and-white checkered floor and colorful decorative vases in the center of each table beckoned her in.

"Cassie!" her friend Aurora called out from behind the counter. "You're back!"

"Back?" Devin murmured, close to her ear.

Her cheeks heated. "I may have stopped by after my PT appointment this morning for a chocolate croissant."

"Hmm, so Cassie Reed has a sweet tooth," Devin mused as he strode up to the counter with Tyler. "Who knew?"

"Me!" Aurora said, patting her chest with a grin. "I knew." She looked back and forth between them, then did a little ta-da flourish toward the chalkboard menu, which listed the prices for gourmet cupcakes, cookies, pastries, tarts and cake slices, as well as a few savory offerings like quiche, croissant sandwiches and sausage rolls. "What can I get you?"

"Devin's never had a macaron."

"Wha-a-a-a-t?" Aurora's eyes went comically wide.

Cassie nudged Devin in the side. "See?"

"What?"

"You're weird."

He laughed. "If you say so."

She turned to Aurora. "I think we need a sampler pack today."

"Ooh, sounds good. How many?"

Cassie bit her lip. At two dollars each, the cost could add up quickly. But Devin took the problem out of her hands by replying, "A dozen. We'll save some for Hailey."

"Perfect," Aurora replied. "Which flavors?"

Devin grinned. "Surprise us."

"But definitely put in some lemon and salted caramel," Cassie interjected. "Oh! And key lime. And pistachio."

Aurora took a pink box off the shelf behind her. "Coming right up."

Devin shifted Tyler from one arm to the other. "You want anything else?" he asked. "Maybe a drink?"

"Are we staying?"

"There's a high chair over there," he said, thrusting his chin toward the seat in question. "Why not?"

"Okay, I'll have a water."

He flashed another smile at Aurora, and Cassie felt an irrational flurry of irritation. "Make that two."

She grabbed the high chair and pulled it over to a table while he paid. Why was she getting annoyed that he was smiling at Aurora? He was only being polite.

And so what if he was flirting with her friend, anyway? Aurora was a catch.

Cassie had already decided there could never be anything between them. He was her little brother's friend, that's all. Her colleague. And soon-to-be next-door neighbor.

Thanks to Jared, that's all they could ever be.

He carried Tyler and their cookies to the table. "Can you grab the waters? They're on the counter. And she said yes to the flyer, by the way. We can bring it over as soon as it's ready."

When Cassie got back to the table, Tyler was strapped into

the high chair and banging his fists on the tray. Devin patted him on the head, then opened the lid to the box of macarons, revealing two rows of the pretty pastel sweets. "Where should we start?"

"I still can't believe you've never had a macaron."

He pulled a yellow cookie out of the box. "Gonna remedy that right now. These are small, though. Are they really worth two bucks a pop?"

"Just wait. You'll see."

He crunched into the cookie.

"Is that the lemon?" she asked, watching his face carefully for his reaction.

He wiped a crumb from the side of his mouth. "No, it's banana."

"Good?" She hadn't tried that flavor yet.

He set the uneaten half of the cookie on a napkin. "It's okay."

"Just okay?" She snatched what was left of it. "May I?"

Amusement tugged at the corners of his lips. "Sure."

She popped the remaining piece of the macaron into her mouth and closed her eyes as the flavor hit. The sweet, crisp shell and the soft, chewy interior. The richness of the white chocolate ganache filling.

So. Good. "You're nuts. That's delicious."

Chuckling, he shrugged. "I don't know. I'm more of a chocolate chip cookie kind of guy. To me, fruit-flavored cookies are usually just…meh."

Cassie plucked another macaron out of the box, determined to find him one he'd like. "Try this one."

He took a bite. Chewed. Swallowed.

"Well?"

He shrugged. "I mean…it's better than the banana, but it's no Reese's."

She plucked what was left of the salted caramel macaron out of his hand. “Give me that.”

Smirking, he leaned back and said, “Be my guest.”

“This is my favorite flavor.”

“You really think the girls will like these?”

“They’ll love them! They’re so good, and they’re colorful and special. They’re also dainty, like the finger sandwiches, so they fit the tea party theme.”

He arched an eyebrow. “But would a mermaid eat them?”

“Without a doubt.”

“Then I guess we’re serving macarons.”

A sparkly feeling shimmered through her at his use of the word “we.” She liked collaborating with Devin. Probably a little too much.

Chapter Six

The morning of Hailey's birthday party, Devin was in the dining hall, up to his elbows in cream cheese and cucumbers.

He cut the crust off another slice of bread. "Are you sure they're going to like these?"

"Yes," Cassie assured him, "cucumber and cream cheese is a classic."

He wrinkled his nose. "And you have to cut them in triangles? What's wrong with squares?"

"Nothing's 'wrong' with them, but that's how you cut her sandwiches for her lunch box, right?"

He nodded.

"So that's not special. Triangles are special."

He closed the sandwich he was working on and rolled up his sleeves. "All these little details."

"It'll all be worth it when you see how happy she is."

"I know." And he did. His daughter's happiness was everything to him. "How's the cake coming along?"

Cassie had baked the cake early this morning so it would have time to cool off before she applied the icing. She took a step back from the counter and waved him closer. "Take a look."

His jaw dropped. "That's incredible." She'd put together a three-layer cake with icing that gradually went from dark blue on the bottom to light blue, then light green, then white on the very top. Little candy pearls and seashells decorated the sides, with a golden mermaid figurine as the centerpiece.

"Thanks."

He truly couldn't believe she'd gone to so much effort for this party. She was special. One of a kind. "It looks too pretty to eat."

"Hopefully the girls won't agree."

"They'll demolish it, I'm sure. Is it a white cake?"

"Yup. And the icing on the inside is buttercream with rainbow sprinkles."

"You thought of everything."

She blushed. "I tried."

"When are you going to change into your fancy mermaid dress?"

"Right before the girls get here. You have the bubble machine set up outside?"

"And the hula hoops. And the beads and string for the bracelets. And the shells."

She rubbed her hands together in anticipation. "This is gonna be fun!"

Tyler let out a squawk from his bouncy seat on the floor. Devin leaned down, unclipped him and hoisted the boy into his arms. "See the pretty cake your mommy made? One day you'll be able to eat yummy cake like that, too."

"Muh muh muh muh muh!" Tyler shouted.

Cassie gasped and rushed to him, her face practically glowing as she lifted him out of Devin's arms. "That's right! I'm your mama!"

"Muh muh muh!" Tyler yelled again.

"Yes, I'm your mama! Good boy!" She kissed his cheek, then gave him a raspberry, making the boy giggle in delight.

"Who's going to watch him during the party?" Devin asked, feeling almost…jealous. Not of the baby, of course, but of the mother-son relationship they had. He wanted Hailey to have a relationship like that with *her* mother, but life had handed her something else entirely.

Cassie smiled. “Aunt Mirriam to the rescue, as always.”

“She’s great, isn’t she? She helped me a lot when Hailey was little.”

“Did she?”

“Whenever Hailey was sick, she’d come over and watch her all day when I was at work. And she’d never accept payment for it, either.”

“I didn’t realize you two were that close.”

“We weren’t. But apparently someone put me on the prayer request list at church back then, and Mirriam took it upon herself to stop by and check in on me. I think she felt bad because she knew my mom had moved to Florida and wasn’t around to help. Told me it’s what Vince would have wanted, for her to step in.”

Boy, was he grateful she’d done it. He’d never be able to repay her for everything she’d done for him—and his new job at the camp was the absolute least of it.

“She and Uncle Vince are the reason I decided to become a foster parent. Remember the kids they took in?”

Devin had vague memories of them bringing a couple different teens to church with them over the years. “Not really. Whatever happened to them?”

“Gustavo got a full-ride scholarship to college. He’s a veterinarian up in Vermont now. He brings his wife and kids down here every summer for vacation.”

“It’s nice that he stayed in touch.”

She gave a humorless laugh. “Better than what happened with Leah, that’s for sure.”

“What happened with her?”

“You don’t remember? She lived with them for almost two years, and they were talking about officially adopting her. But then she ran away. They never heard from her again.”

"Oh, yikes. Now that you mention it, I do kind of remember that. She was Alex's age, right?"

"She was a year younger, but they were in the same grade."

"So you don't know what happened to her?"

Cassie shook her head. "Aunt Mirriam and Uncle Vince looked for her until he passed away, but after that, I think it was just too painful for her to keep going. That's why she was so insistent on installing the security cameras around here. She doesn't want anyone to be able to slip through the cracks like Leah did."

"Aw, man. That's terrible." The thought that a kid could run away and basically vanish into thin air was terrifying. But Devin knew it happened every day. There was so much trouble teens could run into on the streets: drugs, gangs, human trafficking.... He shuddered at the thought of Hailey or Tyler getting mixed up in any of that one day.

And speaking of Tyler, he asked, "Were you hoping for a baby specifically when you applied to be a foster parent?"

Cassie lifted her shoulder. "A baby, a toddler, maybe even a little kid Hailey's age."

"What if they weren't eligible for adoption?"

"I took the classes. I know that reunification is the goal whenever it's possible."

"And you still threw your hat in the ring?"

She shrugged. "Sometimes you have to take a leap of faith."

"Are Tyler's parents working to get him back?"

She placed a few more candy pearls on the cake. "His mother legally surrendered him at a fire station. According to Massachusetts law, that's it. You can't reclaim them after you've surrendered them."

"Whoa. Do you know anything about the circumstances?"

She shook her head. "Not much. She was a teenager, probably gave birth by herself at home. Likely didn't go to the doctor for prenatal care."

Devin winced. "Any complications because of that?"

"He was a little bit on the small side when I first took him home, but as you can see," she said, wiggling his chunky leg, "he caught up quickly."

"Thank God."

"Yes, for sure. I have a lot to be grateful for, don't I, Mr. Dude?" she said, giving Tyler another raspberry.

He giggled again and panted, "Maba, whoba, whee!"

She glanced at the sandwich platter on the counter in front of Devin. "How many do we have now?"

He did a quick count. "Twenty cucumber and cheese, twelve PB and J and twelve cream cheese and strawberry."

"Perfect. That should be enough, right?"

"That's five and a half sandwich quarters each, plus the macarons, the goldfish crackers, the cake and the fruit kebobs. I think we're good."

"How about you put the sandwiches in the fridge, and I'll go get dressed."

"Sounds good. Want me to hang onto Tyler for you?"

"Would you?"

He smiled. "Given what you're doing for me and Hailey today, it's the absolute least I can do."

"All right." She rubbed her hands together. "Give me a few minutes and then let the games begin!"

The tea party—and especially the macarons—had been a big hit with the girls. Now they were outside making bracelets with beads and tiny cowrie seashells while bubbles from the bubble machine floated by.

Most of them had come dressed in pretty blue or green dresses: their mothers' interpretation of mermaid clothes. Cassie, too, was decked out in mermaid paraphernalia. She'd found a modest costume online that hadn't cost much and ordered it. It had cap sleeves, iridescent green sequins and a skirt that hugged her hips but flared out from her knees with layers of tulle that mimicked a mermaid's tail. It had also come with a gold crown, golden wrist cuffs and even a plastic gold trident.

The best part was that there was a matching kids' version, too, so she and Hailey were mermaid twins.

Hailey had squealed with joy when she'd first seen the outfit this morning, and she'd made Devin take about a million pictures of the two of them dressed up in their costumes together.

A couple of the girls' moms had snickered when they'd first seen Cassie, but the others had been kind. She and Devin had prepared coffee and coffee cake for the moms, who were now sitting at a nearby picnic table, chatting and watching their daughters string the beads.

Lisa, a woman Cassie had been friendly with in high school, came over to help her daughter, Avery, with her bracelet. Cassie got up to add more soap to the bubble machine's dispenser, and after a minute, Lisa joined her. "Nice day for this."

Cassie tipped her face up to the sky. "The weather's definitely our friend today."

"Long time, no see." A cheerleader who'd married the mayor's son right out of high school, Lisa now had a classy, stylish vibe. Like one of the rich summer tourists, except she lived here year-round.

"I know. How've you been?"

Lisa waved her hand toward her daughter, the big diamond on her ring finger flashing in the light. "Oh, you know. Mom life is busy, busy."

Cassie's lips quirked up. Finally, she actually did know what mom life was like. "Do you just have the one or…?"

Lisa straightened her shoulders, obviously proud of her kids. "I have three. Avery's my middle child."

"She's adorable."

"Thanks." Lisa leaned closer and lowered her voice. "I heard you got divorced."

Cassie's smile died. "I did."

"And he was a doctor?"

"He was. Still is, I guess." She tried not to pay attention to what Jared was up to these days.

"Shame."

Cassie sighed. "I wish we'd been able to work it out, but he made it clear that he was done."

Empathy sparked in Lisa's eyes. "I've heard those big-city doctors are players. Did he cheat on you?"

Cassie watched one of the bubbles as it rose above the picnic table, shining green and purple in the sunlight before it popped. As far as she knew, he hadn't cheated. But he hadn't been honest with her, either. About his drinking and so many other things.

"He never admitted to anything, but..." Things had never been the same between them after they'd learned she'd never be able to conceive or carry a child. He could have been cheating on her for months, maybe even years.

"Oh, girl. That's the worst. I'm glad you listened to your intuition and kicked him to the curb."

Cassie chewed her lip. "I wasn't actually the one who ended things."

"No? Pshaw. What kind of idiot was he, thinking he could do better than you?"

"Well..." Ugh, this was embarrassing.

"What a snake. Let me guess—he already has a new girlfriend?"

"He's already remarried."

Lisa's eyes bugged. "When did you finalize the divorce?"

"About nine months ago."

"Let me guess again. He went shopping for a younger trophy wife?"

Cassie nodded. Younger, prettier and more fertile, as evidenced by the fact that she was already pregnant.

It stung, for sure, but hopefully she'd learned her lesson: Men couldn't be trusted. They'd say whatever they needed to say to get what they wanted, and as soon as their wants or needs or circumstances changed, they'd be out the door.

Her dad and her brothers were the exception, not the rule.

"His new wife's already pregnant," Cassie admitted.

"Wow. He's going to have his hands full, won't he? How old's *your* baby?"

"He's seven months old now. But he's not Jared's. He's a foster baby."

"Oh, phew. I was going to say, how in the world is he going to cope with Irish twins? For your sake, I'm glad that's not the case. Now you don't have to be tied to him for the rest of your life."

That was something for which Cassie was infinitely grateful. "True."

"So, how'd you get involved with Devin Spencer?"

"Oh." Cassie's heart sped up at Lisa's assumption. "Devin and I aren't involved."

Confusion flashed across Lisa's face. "Is he paying you to run this party?"

Cassie shook her head. "No, we work together. Here at the camp."

More confusion. "I thought the camp was closed?"

"We're reopening it. Me, Devin and my brothers."

"Really? I had no idea." Lisa glanced around, gesturing toward the forest and the pond. "It's a great spot. Will it be a day camp? Overnight camp?"

"Overnight."

"Will it be open this summer? We'd send my oldest."

"We're working on it. Interviewing potential counselors, getting the activities all set up. I'll give you a flyer before you leave."

"Perfect. And working with Devin must be fun." She threw

a glance at the picnic table, where the man in question was currently topping off various moms' coffees. "Most of the moms from the kids' class think he's great."

"*Most* of them?"

Lisa grimaced. "There are always some people who're obsessed with dredging up people's missteps from the past."

Ah, the drinking. Funny how the thing she'd been so concerned about just a few weeks ago didn't really faze her that much anymore.

However, there were still plenty of other reasons they could never be together. "Sounds like you already know he used to party a lot."

"Well, not anymore. You know this town. Word gets around fast, and I would've heard. But people do talk about how he's a really great dad."

Cassie's gaze sprang to Hailey, who was up out of her seat and asking Devin to help her put on her new bracelet. "He is a great dad."

"And Hailey's the sweetest. So polite. I love that you've got matching outfits. I used to do that with Avery all the time. Just wait for the holidays—that girl will be so happy to have you around. I've always thought it was super sad that she doesn't really have a mom."

Were the matching outfits too much? Had Cassie inadvertently veered into mom territory? Devin hadn't seemed concerned about it, but would the moms at the picnic table draw the same conclusion Lisa had? That she and Devin were involved, and that she was angling to become Hailey's stepmom?

Clearly, Cassie needed to take a giant step back. She didn't want to give anyone the wrong idea.

Especially herself.

Chapter Seven

"Daddy." Hailey pulled on Devin's sleeve.

He came awake with a start, disoriented. He must have dozed off while watching the hockey game in his new living room. Who knew a mermaid tea party would take so much out of him? "What is it, peanut?"

His daughter was still dressed in her mermaid clothes. If he left it up to her, she'd probably sleep in them, too. "I want to open my presents. Can we please, please, please go see if Miss Cassie's home yet?" Right before the party, Mirriam had come to camp to pick up Tyler so that Cassie could focus on the girls. Which meant that after the party, Cassie had needed to go and retrieve him.

He glanced at his watch. Almost eight. "It's getting late, Hailey. She might have already put Tyler down to sleep."

"But you said we could ask her!"

"I know, but I didn't expect her to stay out so long." When Hailey had first asked him about it earlier, he'd said sure, they could save the big unwrapping until Cassie came over. He'd thought she'd just pop over to Mirriam's to pick up Tyler and come right back.

"Maybe she's back! You were sleeping for a long time! You even snored!"

He chuckled. He was well aware that he snored. Sometimes, his own snoring woke him up. "Why don't we open the presents on our own and you can show them to Miss Cassie tomorrow?"

Hailey's little face creased in a frown. "That's no fun, Daddy. I want her to see me open them."

"What if I take a video? Then you can show her tomorrow."

"No, I want her here with me now!"

"Hailey. She might not be able to come over right now."

"It's not fair. If she comes over, she can see my presents and brush my hair before bed. Why can't we just *ask*?"

"Fine," he said, hefting himself out of his comfy leather armchair. It fit perfectly with the cabin's wooden beams and gray stone fireplace. It was rustic here, and he loved it. Living at the camp made him feel like a frontiersman, an adventurer who lived off his wits and his wilderness skills, even though he was still a modern guy who drove a truck and shopped for his groceries and helped his daughter brush her hair. "We'll go ask."

Hailey took his hand and practically dragged him to the front door. "If Tyler's sleeping, we can bring my presents over to their house!"

There had been seven little guests at the party, so it wouldn't be too much hassle to carry the gifts next door to Cassie's place. "Only if Miss Cassie's okay with it, peanut. We don't want to intrude."

"Daddy." Hailey put her hands on her hips, as though she couldn't believe he could be this dense. "Everybody loves *presents*!"

"Everybody loves their own presents, silly pants. Not everyone will be jumping up and down to watch *you* open *your* presents."

"Miss Cassie will. I know it."

He hoped she was right. He'd texted Shannon earlier to remind her that it was Hailey's birthday, but so far she'd been radio silent. He'd hate it if a second woman let Hailey down today, too.

Outside, the sun had just set, and twilight was settling over the camp. The sound of waves lapping the shore was a constant here, although there wasn't much wind tonight, so the ocean's roar was muted. The marsh was teeming with peeper frogs, and even though it wasn't full dark, they were already starting to call out, as were the crickets. In a couple of hours, they'd start hearing the owls.

Hailey ran up the steps to Cassie's cabin and knocked.

For a long minute, there was no response. Hailey looked up at Devin with a pout. "Her car's here."

"Tyler might be in the bathtub, or she might be rocking him to sleep. We don't want to bother them. Let's go home."

"No." Hailey gave her head a firm shake. "I wanna wait."

"Come on, honey bunny. It's time to go. You've had a big day."

"Daddy," she whined, stomping her foot, "no. I don't want to leave without seeing Miss Cassie."

"Hailey," he said, getting stern. "Do I need to pick you up and carry you back home?"

"Where is she?" Hailey cried. "I want to see her! It's not fair!"

"Shh," he said, reaching for her.

She darted away from him. "Daddy! Daddy! No!"

The door flew open, and Devin straightened, embarrassed that he hadn't been able to nip this tantrum in the bud before Cassie could witness it.

"Everything okay out here?" Cassie asked, a furrow on her brow. She wasn't in her mermaid dress anymore, but faded jeans and a gray sweatshirt. Devin had liked the mermaid dress a lot, but he liked this look on her, too.

"You're here! You're here!" Hailey screamed, throwing herself at Cassie.

"Oof! Hey, cutie." She leaned down and gave Hailey a hug. "Good to see you, too."

"Come watch me open my presents!"

"You know what, sweetie? Tyler just went to sleep, so I can't come over right now."

"See, peanut? I told y—"

"We can bring my presents here!" Hailey interrupted. "Daddy said."

"Oh." Cassie widened her eyes at him. "Did he now?"

Devin winced. "I told her we could ask."

"So, can we? Can we bring them over? I really want you to be there when I open them!"

Cassie gave Devin a long, unreadable look, and he wished he knew what she was thinking. Hailey wasn't normally this pushy. On one hand, he wanted to squash her bad behavior, but on the other, it was her birthday and she wanted to share her excitement with her new friend.

Finally, Cassie moved her attention to Hailey. "Can you be very quiet?"

"Yes! Yes, yes, yes! I'll be quieter than—than a bee!"

Devin smothered a laugh. *A bee?*

"That sounds good," Cassie said seriously. "Bees are very quiet."

"All they do is buzz," Hailey explained. "We learned about them in school. But I won't even buzz! I'll be super duper silent!"

"Perfect." Cassie waved them inside.

Devin let Hailey go in while he popped back over to their cabin to grab the gifts. When he got back to Cassie's, she and Hailey were at the kitchen table, enjoying leftover macarons from the party. She'd been right about those little cookies; the girls had loved them.

The layouts of their cabins were the same, but hers was cozier. She had a rug under her kitchen table, framed photos on many of her shelves and prints with little sayings like *Difficult Roads Lead to Beautiful Destinations* and *Choose Joy* hanging on the walls.

Hailey hopped up to go wash her hands in the bathroom, giving him a moment alone with Cassie. "Hey, sorry about this. She insisted we come over and see if you wanted in on the gift-opening extravaganza, but we didn't mean to put you out."

"It's fine. Tyler's sleeping anyway."

"And I know I said it earlier, but thanks again for today. Best party she's ever had. She won't stop talking about it."

"It was my pleasure."

Devin hesitated for a split second, but then decided to shoot his shot. Cassie Reed was *still* the full package, and the way she'd stepped up to host his daughter's birthday had made it clear that Hailey would welcome her into her life with open arms. "Can I take you out to dinner sometime to say thank you?"

Cassie shook her head. "That's not necessary."

Devin leaned forward a little, catching her eye at the same time that he caught the hint of her perfume: coconuts, roses and vanilla, all rolled up into one. "I know it's not *necessary*, but I'd like to."

Uneasiness flickered across her face, and she looked away. "I don't think that's a good idea."

"Are you sure? I've been meaning to try Half Shell for a long time, and it'd be fun to go with you." Half Shell was a fancy seafood restaurant in Wychmere Bay that had just earned itself a Michelin Star.

"Devin." She chewed her lip. "As what? Neighbors? Coworkers? Friends?"

Hmm, it wasn't a great sign that she was trying to box him into one of those categories, but he'd never been a guy who gave up easily. He flashed her the grin that used to work for him in college. "How about we start with friends and see where it goes?"

She started to shake her head, but then Hailey bounced back into the room, cutting off her rejection midstream.

For now, Devin would take the interruption.

In time, hopefully he could change her mind.

Cassie stared at Tyler's caseworker in disbelief. They were in a conference room at the office of the Department of Children & Families in Hyannis, which was cramped and too warm. Cassie adjusted Tyler on her lap, and he laughed and bounced up and down, oblivious to the gravity of the situation. "I don't understand. You said there was no father."

The caseworker, Lianne, gave her a sympathetic smile. "There wasn't. He didn't know about the baby. Until now."

"But..." Cassie's voice wobbled. Oh, boy. *Don't cry, don't cry, don't cry.*

"Look." Lianne leaned forward in her chair. "Nothing's concrete yet. He's filed to establish parentage, but that's it. It hasn't gone to court yet, and when it does, the judge might not rule in his favor, especially since the sixty-day window has passed. I just wanted you to be prepared."

Cassie took a deep breath. "Okay."

"And to understand why we're tabling the new home study until this matter is resolved."

"You don't want to do the home study?" Cassie felt her voice wobble again. Lianne had already done the interviews and reference checks, but she needed to come back and assess Cassie's new home at the camp before the adoption process could move forward.

"We do," Lianne assured her, "but it's a lot of work, and if the judge rules that a paternity test is in the child's best interest..."

Fear morphed into anger. "You're going to hand Tyler over,

just like that? Who even is this guy? How do you know that he's a good person, or that he'd be a good dad?"

Lianne straightened in her seat, empathy receding. "Look, we're always going to do what's best for the child. Sometimes that's adoption, sometimes that's reunification. If you feel like the situation is too much for you, we can always move Tyler to a new placement until this matter has been resolved."

Cassie's heart rate spiked. "No! That's not what I'm—no. Leave him with me. Please. Moving to a new family will be hard on him. I understand it might eventually come to that, but for now, please just leave him with me."

Lianne sighed. "I know this isn't the news you were hoping for, but sometimes we're only meant to be in a child's life for a season."

Cassie nodded mutely. If that were true about Tyler, why did she have a hollow the size of the Grand Canyon in the middle of her chest?

Chapter Eight

"So," Aunt Mirriam said, looking first at Cassie, then at Devin, Jonah and Alex, "are we ready? Can we do it?"

Aunt Mirriam had pulled off the impossible. She'd almost completely filled Camp Piper's schedule for September and October with school groups, church groups, a Scouting group and a bunch of teenage foster kids from a group home in Boston. The only catch was that the group home wanted to do a day trip first to make sure the camp would meet its needs for a longer stay in the fall.

"It has to be *this* Saturday?" Cassie asked, wringing her hands. They were in the dining hall, which looked phenomenal now that Devin had finished not just cleaning it, but refurbishing it, too: rows of rustic picnic tables sat under the high-vaulted wood ceiling, while framed, old-timey maritime maps graced the walls.

"Yes, honey," Aunt Mirriam said. "They had some indoor rock-climbing event set up, but the gym was flooded. They need something to fill the gap."

"It's just so fast." Ever since her meeting with Tyler's social worker, Cassie had felt fearful and unfocused. But this was a great opportunity, and it would be good to get the foster kids confirmed for the fall.

"We're ready, though," Devin said. "Cassie and I can put together a fun agenda for the kids, no problem."

Cassie shot him a skeptical look, and he sent her a furrowed brow in return, as though to say, *Why are you being so negative?*

She didn't like it, but she couldn't help it. Jared had pulled the rug out from under her once, and now the social worker was doing it again, but in slow motion. How long would it be before the paternity suit went to court? How long was she supposed to live in limbo?

And if she couldn't keep Tyler forever, then how long did she have?

Glancing at where he was sleeping in his car seat, she almost wished he'd wake up just so she could sneak in a cuddle.

"How many kids should we plan for?" Devin asked.

"Not that many," Aunt Mirriam replied. "There's twelve of them."

"Okay, then that should be easy. We'll break them into two groups and rotate through some different activities. The water's not warm enough yet for swimming, but we can take them kayaking, do some arts and crafts, have a big volleyball game, do a campfire. It'll be a great trial run for the open house."

"Wonderful," Aunt Mirriam said. "I'll let them know." She took out her phone as though to alert them immediately, then waved goodbye.

After a minute, Cassie, Jonah, Alex and Devin, who'd volunteered to carry Tyler's car seat, followed her out to the parking lot.

"I can be here on Saturday," Jonah offered.

"Me, too," Alex said. "Call me if you need anything before then."

Devin nodded, then set down the car seat so he could shake her brothers' hands before they headed off.

They pulled out of their parking spots, and Cassie breathed a sigh of relief. She'd seen them both at church this morning, but she hadn't filled them in on the new development with

Tyler. She wanted to tell her parents first, but it was hard to reach them on their cruise. Plus, she was kind of hoping that if she ignored it, the whole situation would just…disappear.

Lord, I don't know if I can do this. Why would You give him to me only to take him away?

Steeling herself, she decided she couldn't dwell on the what-ifs. Moving forward in faith was the only way she'd get through this.

She'd tried that, though, with Jared, and it hadn't worked; it had only delayed the inevitable and given her false hope in the lead-up to the divorce.

This will be different, Lord, won't it? It has to be. Please.

Devin scrubbed a hand through his hair. "Well, this'll be interesting."

"Yeah."

He turned to her, squinting against the sun. "Everything okay?"

"Fine." She folded her arms across her chest, then realized it made her look defensive and let them fall back to her sides. "Why?"

"You seem worried. If there's something about camp you think we need to fix before Saturday—"

"It's not about camp."

"But there is *something* you're worried about?"

A cloud passed by the sun, casting them both in shadow. "I don't want to talk about it."

He studied her for a long moment, his jaw angled to the side. "This isn't about the other night, is it? I'm sorry if I made you uncomfortable asking you out to dinner."

She let her breath out in a whoosh. If only her anxiety was about his dinner invitation and the precedent it might set. "Oh, no, don't worry. It's not about that."

"You're sure?"

"Totally." It was flattering, actually, to know that the attraction she felt wasn't one-sided. Not that it could go anywhere. For all the obvious reasons, plus the big secret she carried around with her like a stone.

"'Cause I'd hate it if I was the one making *you* walk on eggshells," he said, his gaze earnest and intense.

"This has nothing to do with you. I promise."

Tyler made a noise in his sleep, and they both turned to look at him, but then he settled and went slack once again in his car seat. "Buddy's really taking a good nap today, huh?" Devin asked.

"I'll take the peace and quiet when I can get it."

He chuckled. "I feel the same way when Hailey's over at a friend's house."

"Is that where she is this afternoon?"

"Yup. She and her friend Avery go to Sunday school together. She tags along to their house quite a bit."

"Avery's mom and I were in the same class at school."

"That's cool. Lisa's good people."

Cassie nodded, but she still felt unsettled. What would she do on afternoons like this if she lost custody of Tyler? Life without him would be so empty. Wasn't it enough that she'd lost her marriage? Did she really have to lose her son, too?

Devin was watching her, his gray eyes full of concern. "Do you want to come over for a few minutes? Have a cup of coffee?"

"That's okay," she said, hating the shakiness of her voice. It was obvious that Devin could tell something was wrong, no matter how hard she tried to hide it. "But thank you."

"We've got macarons."

A smile played around the edges of her mouth. He certainly had her number. *Feeling blue? Just add sugar.* "Do you?"

"Turns out Hailey loves them. The girl's got expensive taste."

"You mean great taste."

"Sure, boss. That's exactly what I mean."

Cassie rolled her eyes, but the nickname was a good reminder that they could never be more than co-workers, neighbors and friends. "What flavors do you have?"

"All of them. I got another sampler pack."

"Ooh. Well then, by all means, lead the way."

Smirking, he gave her a jaunty salute, picked up Tyler's car seat like it weighed nothing and motioned for her to follow him.

Which she did. For the macarons.

And maybe also so he could remind her that, even if she lost Tyler, her life wouldn't be completely empty. She had people in her corner.

If she weren't so afraid they'd let her down like Jared, maybe she'd even let them in.

Tyler woke up as soon as Devin set his car seat down inside his cabin. He was happy, though, and Devin played with him on the carpet while Cassie ran next door to get him a bottle.

"Buh, buh, buh, buh," Tyler babbled, rocking back and forth on his hands and knees.

"You want your bottle?" Devin asked, right down there with him.

"Buh buh."

"Bo-ttle," Devin enunciated.

"Buh buh." Tyler lay down on his stomach and rolled onto his back, catching one of his feet and bringing it to his mouth.

"Don't eat your toes, dude." Devin reached out to gently remove the boy's chubby foot from his mouth. It never ceased to amaze him how flexible babies could be. "Germs."

"Guh guh."

"That's right. Germs."

Tyler rolled onto his stomach again and got back up on his hands and knees. He was wearing a blue-and-white-striped onesie with short sleeves, plus a pair of baby jeans with an elastic waist. "You really want to crawl, don't you?"

"Cuh cuh."

"Crawl."

Tyler looked at him and laughed. His eyes were so big. Devin had read somewhere that newborns' eyes were about sixty-five percent of their adult size, while their heads were only twenty-five percent of the size they'd grow into, so it made sense. Proportionally, babies' eyes *were* quite big for their tiny faces.

"Come on, man." Devin modeled crawling for the little guy. "You're slacking."

"Suh, suh, suh, suh," Tyler said, kicking his feet up toward the ceiling.

"Slack-er," Devin enunciated, then gave the boy's tummy a tickle.

Tyler squealed in delight.

"What're you two doing?" Cassie asked, hip propped against the doorway, bottle in hand.

"You know." Devin grinned at her. "Guy stuff."

She shook her finger at him, mocking sternness. "You'd better not be teaching him how to crawl. We haven't recovered from him learning how to sit up by himself yet."

Devin laughed. He remembered when Hailey had first learned how to sit on her own. She'd wake up screaming in the night because she'd sit up in her crib but couldn't figure out how to get herself back down. "Oh, really? You're sitting all by yourself now, man?"

"Suh suh," Tyler said.

"Sitting," Devin replied.

Cassie smirked. "Babies don't start learning words until they're almost a year old."

"What can I say? Either he's a prodigy, or I'm a great teacher."

"Delusional is more like it."

He gave her a lofty look. "You're just jealous he was talking to me and not to you."

"Mm-hmm," she drawled, fighting a smile. Devin smiled back, glad that she didn't seem sad anymore. He was, however, still curious about what was going on.

"Sit," he said, motioning to his couch with his chin. "I'll hand him up to you."

She sat and shook the bottle. Devin hefted Tyler into his arms and then brought him over to her. The boy squealed and clapped when he saw what Cassie was holding, then practically tried to shimmy out of Devin's grasp. "Buh, buh, buh," he panted.

"Yes, honey, I have your bottle," Cassie said, opening her arms for him.

He settled onto her lap, laying his head in the crook of her elbow, and opened his mouth like a baby bird. Cassie gave him the bottle, and he started draining it like a champ.

Devin plopped down in his leather armchair. "I swear he's trying to talk."

Cassie sighed. "I wish."

Devin gave her a funny look. Yes, it would be fun if Tyler started talking, but she sounded more serious than whimsical. "What's up, Cass? Talk to me."

She looked down at Tyler gulping his formula for a long moment. "I had a meeting with Tyler's caseworker the other day. They're putting the adoption on hold."

"What? Why?"

"His…a man came forward and is petitioning the court to establish that he's the father."

Devin's jaw dropped. "Wow. I thought you said Tyler was abandoned at a fire station."

"He was."

"So how did this guy even find him?"

"I have no idea."

"And they're halting the adoption because of it?"

Tyler finished his bottle, and Cassie placed him in a sitting position on the floor. He let out a loud belch, and Devin chuckled while Cassie shook her head in amusement. "Men. You guys never grow out of the potty humor, do you?"

Devin shrugged. "That was a big burp."

"Buh buh."

"Yup," Devin said to the baby. "Burp."

"Don't teach him how to say that!"

"Why not? It's a real word."

"I don't want his first word to be 'burp'!"

"He was calling his bottle buh-buh, too, so I think you're safe for the time being."

"So you admit it? He's just babbling? Not responding to your phenomenal teaching?"

Devin winked at her. "Did you just call me phenomenal?"

"You called *yourself* phenomenal."

"I never called myself phenomenal. I said I was a great teacher. Big difference. But I'll take it."

Cassie rolled her eyes, but she was smiling. "Of course you will."

"Back to the matter at hand. They're canceling the adoption on you?"

Her face shut down. "No. Not yet. But they're putting it on hold while all of this goes through family court."

"I thought you said you couldn't get a baby back after you'd abandoned it."

"You can't. Not here in Massachusetts. But it wasn't the father who surrendered him at the fire station, it was the mother, so apparently this guy *can* apply to establish paternity. Usually they won't let you do it unless it's within sixty days of the surrender, but his lawyer is claiming extenuating circumstances. I guess they're going to hear him out."

"Ugh. That's frustrating."

"Yeah, and when I expressed that frustration to the caseworker, she threatened to move Tyler to a new foster family."

"Oh, no."

"I took it back right away and told her I could handle it, but Devin..." She glanced down at Tyler, who had half of his right fist stuffed in his mouth. "I honestly don't know if I can."

He scooted to the very edge of his chair, leaning as close to her as he could get without touching her. "You can, Cass. You're strong. You stared down an SUV to protect my daughter, and then look at how fast you bounced back from that knee injury. And hopefully it'll all come to nothing, anyway, and the adoption'll go through just like you planned."

She shook her head. "I'm not that strong. I stayed with Jared despite his drinking even though he lied to me from the get-go. I just—I took my vows seriously, you know? But then he left anyway, and he slid right into his fancy new life like it was no big deal, and I was left standing on the side of the road, reeling."

Devin blew out a breath. Man. Her ex-husband had been a drinker. No wonder she'd reacted so badly to the idea of working with him when Mirriam had first hired him.

"When I got the call about Tyler, it felt like a lifeline. But what if it's not? What if it's just another way for God to kick me in the face?"

"Kick you in the...? No. That's not how it works, Cass. Not at all." He was tempted to share his life verse with her—*He only is my rock and my salvation: He is my defence; I shall not be moved*—but decided that she wasn't really in the headspace to hear it.

"How does it work, then? You tell me. Because I thought I had everything figured out, but then the divorce turned everything I thought I knew on its head."

Tyler, on the carpet, laughed. He had one of his feet in his mouth again.

"I'm sorry about your divorce. Your ex sounds like an idiot."

"He wasn't all bad. And when push came to shove, he had his reasons."

"I find that hard to believe." If there was one thing Devin had learned from his years of attending Celebrate Recovery meetings, it was that people who struggled with addictive behavior always had an excuse.

Just like he had, as a teenager and a college student, telling himself he had the right to let off steam and party because his parents had lied to him by keeping his adoption a secret for so long.

"Let me guess—he told you he worked hard? That he deserved to relax with a drink at the end of a long day?"

She lifted her shoulder. "I mean, kind of? But I wasn't even talking about the drinking."

His brow furrowed in confusion. "Then what were you talking about?"

"I—You know what? Never mind."

"Come on, Cass. Don't leave me hanging."

"It's…it's personal."

"Whatever you think you did to deserve his bad behavior, I can pretty much guarantee it's not as embarrassing as getting married in Vegas on a drunken whim."

A little hand patted his foot, and Devin's gaze shot down to Tyler, who was lying on his tummy, smacking Devin's toes with his open palm. "How'd you get all the way over here, bud? Did you crawl?"

Tyler smiled up at him, drool dripping down his chin. "Cuh, cuh, cuh."

"He probably just rolled," Cassie said. "Otherwise, I'd have noticed."

"Did you roll, buddy? Or did you crawl?"

"It's too early for him to crawl."

"I don't know, Cass. I think he might've crawled. He was getting close earlier."

"Rocking back and forth on his hands and knees? He's been doing that for weeks."

"At some point, they graduate from the rocking to the actual crawling. Today might be the day."

"No, there's no way I missed his first time crawling because I was busy talking to you."

"Thanks," he said dryly. "Thanks a lot."

She gave him a pert look. "You know I didn't mean it like that."

Devin reached down and flipped Tyler around so he was facing Cassie. "Crawl to your mama, bud. Show her you can do it."

The baby giggled and fell back onto his tummy, then rolled three times.

"Oh, sure. Make me a liar."

Cassie snickered. "Told you."

"Okay, fine. You were right. About the crawling. But not about your ex. He was an idiot, and whatever mitigating factors you think exist, I don't care. But if you ever want to tell me about them, I'm more than just a pretty face. I'll listen."

"Puh puh," Tyler said.

"See? Tyler agrees with me." He pointed at his face. "Pretty."

Smiling, she shook her head. "Tyler's babbling. And rolling. Not talking. Or crawling."

He made a *bring it* gesture with his hands. "Go ahead. Rub it in."

She laughed. "Didn't you promise me macarons?"

"Say less." Devin jumped to his feet, ready to retrieve the treats.

One of these days, he'd earn Cassie's trust. Until then, he'd settle for bringing that gorgeous smile to her face as many times as he possibly could.

Chapter Nine

The foster kids were coming to camp on Saturday, and since Devin and Cassie were going to take them kayaking, they needed to familiarize themselves with their route.

Tyler, obviously, wasn't taking the trip with them, but Hailey had the day off due to a professional development day at her school, and she was so excited she was skipping down the path to the beach, the sequins on her shirt sparkling with every step.

Cassie was right behind her, carrying the life jackets and the paddles. Devin was in the rear, bringing the first of the kayaks from the boat rack in the storage shed to the water. When they got to the shore, he gently deposited the boat on the sand.

"I could have managed that one," Cassie said.

He gave her a little smirk that seemed to say *not on my watch*, and she shrugged. If she didn't have to carry a fifty-pound boat on her shoulders, she wasn't going to complain.

"Keep an eye on Hailey while I get the tandem?"

"Of course."

"Be right back."

"Hailey," Cassie called out. She was trying her best not to think about what might happen with Tyler. She was trying not to let fear rule, trying to trust God that everything would work out the way it was supposed to. "Come put on your life jacket."

The girl skipped over and plucked the small yellow life jacket off the sand. "Daddy said we can go see the seals!"

"If they're there today, we can."

"I love the seals! They're so cute!"

Cute wasn't necessarily the first word Cassie would use to describe the big, blubbery animals, but they were fun to look at, that was for sure. Listening to them bark, however? That was something she could live without.

Hailey zipped up her life jacket and Cassie tightened the straps for her, then put on her own flotation device. Devin set the tandem kayak down next to the single and did a twirly hand gesture followed by a bow. "Hailey, your chariot awaits."

"Daddy, can I ride with Miss Cassie?"

A flash of surprise illuminated his face. "No, you stay with me, peanut. It'll be easier for me to paddle us both around than it'll be for Miss Cassie."

"I'm a good paddler! I'll help!"

"I know you will, but little girl muscles aren't as big or strong as dad muscles."

"What about Miss Cassie muscles? She carries Tyler around all the time, and he's gigantic!"

Cassie dipped her head to hide her smile. She wasn't a weakling, but she was nowhere near as strong as Devin. "How about you start with your dad, and then you and I can go out together at the end if you still want to?"

Hailey pouted for a second, then nodded. "Fine."

"Dad's kinda boring, huh?" Cassie asked, lips twitching. Devin, in return, shot her a wry look.

"No, he's not boring." Hailey hooked her arms around Devin's waist. "He's fun! But he can't do French braids. And he's bad at making bracelets. And you and me are mermaid twins, Miss Cassie, so we should be together in the sea!"

Devin covered his eyes with his hand, shaking with silent laughter.

"We should have worn our costumes, shouldn't we? That was a missed opportunity."

"We can wear them later, when we get home! And you can braid my hair!"

"Sounds like a plan."

"Well, now that *that's* settled…" Devin grabbed Hailey under her armpits and swung her into the kayak, then pushed it into the water before he hopped in. "Come on, Cass," he called out. "Time's a-wasting."

Wearing her water shoes, she ran into the surf with her kayak, then jumped into her seat. "Brr." The water was freezing—probably around fifty degrees—and she was only wearing a T-shirt and shorts because she knew she was going to get wet.

"You okay?" Devin asked.

"Yup. Let's get moving so I can warm up."

They started paddling. It was an overcast day, but the clouds weren't heavy—she doubted it would rain. Hailey sang and dipped her paddle into the water every now and then, but it was clear that Devin was doing the lion's share of the work for the tandem. Cassie hadn't been out on the water like this in a long time, and she was surprised she was keeping up as well as she was. She was also surprised she wasn't splashing herself more as she paddled.

"I don't think I've been out on a kayak in, like, five years."

"Really?" Devin said. "It's the first time this year for us, but we went a few times last summer, didn't we, Hailey?"

"Daddy taught me surfing last summer, too!"

"Oh, that's fun. Were you good at it?"

"Uh-huh."

"She's a natural," Devin said, resting his paddle on his thighs for a moment so he could wipe a couple of water droplets off his face.

"That makes perfect sense, seeing as she's a mermaid princess and all."

Hailey giggled. Devin put his paddle back into the water, and Cassie did her best to keep up. Twenty minutes later, they pointed their kayaks to shore next to the Sandpiper Cove pier.

American flags waved in the wind every ten feet or so along the wooden boardwalk. It wasn't a super touristy area at this time of year, but there were a few little shops and restaurants tucked in between the ticket booths for a whale watching tour and a parasailing company. Sailboats, motorboats and even a couple of commercial fishing boats were docked in the harbor today.

As they pulled their kayaks onto the sand, Cassie glanced at the clam shack on the pier. It had been a hot minute since she'd had fried seafood, and suddenly the thought of a crispy piece of battered cod dipped in tangy tartar sauce was making her mouth water. "Do you like fish and chips, Hailey?"

The little girl clapped her hands. "Ooh, yes!"

"Let's go," Cassie said, smiling at Devin. "My treat." She'd brought her phone and a credit card in a waterproof pouch she was wearing around her neck.

"All right. But you'll have to let me get dessert."

"Ice cream, Daddy. We're going to get ice cream, right?" Hailey asked, her hands in the *pretty please* position.

"We're going to let Miss Cassie choose what she'd like."

Hailey turned her pleading eyes on her. "Ice cream, Miss Cassie. You know it's the best dessert in the whole wide world!"

Cassie narrowed her eyes to feign deep thought. "What about macarons? Or cake?"

"We have macarons at home! And leftover cake, too!"

"But no ice cream?"

Hailey gave her head a vigorous shake. "No, Daddy doesn't buy it because he says he'll eat it all in one sitting."

Cassie sent Devin an amused look. “Did Hailey just disclose your kryptonite?”

He shrugged. “I like ice cream. It’s no big secret.”

“Favorite flavor?”

“Butter pecan or pistachio. Or maple walnut. Depends on the day.”

Cassie wrinkled her nose. “The nutty ones. Of course.”

“Oh, come on. Don’t tell me you don’t like Reese’s.”

“Who doesn’t like Reese’s? Nuts and *chocolate* are perfectly acceptable.”

He laughed. “But nuts and sugar don’t cut it?”

She shook her head. “Not even close. What about you, Hailey? What’s your favorite flavor?”

“Bubblegum! And cookie dough! And mint chocolate chip!”

“I like all those, too.” Cassie held her hand out for a fist bump, and Hailey tapped her knuckles. “But fudge brownie’s my favorite.”

“Toppings?” Devin asked.

“Now that you mention it, I wouldn’t say no to Reese’s peanut butter sauce. Or M&Ms. Or whipped cream. Or a maraschino cherry.” Her stomach growled just thinking about the deliciousness all of that would entail.

“I love whipped cream!” Hailey chirped. “But Daddy never buys it.”

Cassie put her hands on her hips in mock disapproval. “Your dad needs to get with the program, doesn’t he?”

“Yeah, Daddy. Get us more whipped cream!”

“You two are ganging up on me now? Fantastic.” He was smiling as he said it, though, so it was clear he didn’t really mind.

Hailey latched onto Cassie’s hand and started tugging her toward the clam shack. “Let’s go get lunch, ’cause after lunch, we can have ice cream!”

Chuckling, Cassie let herself be pulled along. She was glad they were neighbors. She wanted to have this sweet little girl in her life for many years to come.

Cassie didn't even make it through half of her sundae, but Devin had every last bite of his waffle cone. The maple walnut ice cream was just as good as he'd remembered. Better, even, because Cassie was there, teasing him about his poor taste in ice cream while she spooned up sugary bites of her own chocolatey treat.

Hailey had a sundae, too: bubblegum ice cream with strawberry sauce, pink sprinkles, marshmallows and whipped cream. Unsurprisingly, his daughter now had melted ice cream all over her face.

"Go wash up in the bathroom, silly pants. You are a *mess*."

"Daddy," she replied, trying to scrape another spoonful of ice cream out of her very empty cup. "I'm not finished yet."

"You want some of mine, Hailey?" Cassie asked, tipping her sundae toward his daughter.

Hailey looked at the soupy mess Cassie was holding. "Mmm, no thanks." She glanced at Devin. "I'm done now."

"Good girl. Throw your cup away and go wash up."

While the ice cream shop in Wychmere Bay was decorated like a 1950s soda shop, the Sandpiper Cove Creamery had leaned into its beachfront location. Seascape murals featuring dolphins, jellyfish and lobsters covered three of the walls. Colorful fishing buoys hung from the ceiling. There was even a fish tank with exotic tropical fish on display near the back windows.

"Thanks for the ice cream," Cassie said.

"Thank *you* for lunch." His gaze locked with hers, and his temperature shot up. She was so pretty like this: windswept hair, casual clothes, ice-cream-powered smile. He wanted to do this again sometime, just the two of them. But he'd asked her out the other day and she'd declined, and he didn't think that he'd had enough time yet to change her mind.

"Any word about what's going on with Tyler?"

She looked away. "No."

"I don't understand why the social worker told you about it if they're not sure the case is going to move forward."

"I don't, either. Maybe she thought it would give me time to mentally prepare in case things don't work out, but I don't know. All it's really doing is making me anxious. Sometimes ignorance is bliss."

He hated hearing that she was anxious. "If it helps, I've been praying for you. For both of you."

"Thanks. I've been praying, too, but I'll admit that my prayers are all pretty selfish. He's been with me for almost his entire life. How can taking him away and giving him to a stranger be the best thing for him?"

"Well—" Devin scratched his ear "—it would be his dad, so would he really be a stranger?"

She pursed her lips. "Considering he's never even met Tyler, yes. He's a stranger. And will he really be equipped to raise a baby? If the mom was a teenager, he can't be that much older himself."

"Yeah, that'd be tough." He had to bite his tongue to stop himself from telling her that he'd only been twenty when Hailey was born. It was clear from her current state of mind that she didn't want to hear it.

But for him? He could see why the kid might want to fight for custody.

And yet, of course he could understand why Cassie would want to fight for Tyler, too.

Chapter Ten

Paddling home was a lot more difficult for Cassie than paddling to the pier. She had blisters on her hands now, and her arms and shoulders were already starting to get sore.

Plus, the clouds had gotten heavier over lunch, and the wind had picked up. The afternoon was definitely threatening rain.

Devin and Hailey got a few feet ahead, and then Devin let Hailey take over until Cassie caught up. "You okay there, boss?"

Cassie blew a strand of hair out of her face as she huffed out a mirthless laugh. "I'll survive."

"What's wrong?"

"My hands are a little beat up." She held out one of her palms so he could see. "And my arms are getting sore."

He winced at the sight of her blisters. "Hailey, do you think you can hold onto Miss Cassie's paddle so we can tow her?"

"No, no," Cassie said, dropping her raised palm down to her paddle. "It's not that bad." The thought of Devin having to tow her to shore was humiliating. Especially after what he'd said at the ice cream parlor—that Tyler's father wouldn't really be a stranger.

Technically, of course, he was right. But he'd raised the subject as though he'd be a sympathetic ear, and then…he hadn't been.

All she'd wanted to do was vent, and he'd pulled the logic card on her.

"Come on," Devin cajoled. "Hand one end of your paddle to Hailey. I don't mind."

"Well, maybe I do." Gritting her teeth against the burn of her blisters, she started paddling again. It was the principle of the thing. If she couldn't count on herself, who could she count on? No one.

Not even five minutes later, it started to rain. It wasn't a light misting, either, but big, fat drops that plopped into the boat and quickly soaked her hair and clothes.

The waves got choppier, making it harder to progress toward home. Whitecaps tipped over the rim of her kayak, joining the inch or so of rainwater that was sloshing around in the bottom of her boat.

A flash of lightning lit up the clouds, and then a long, deep growl of thunder echoed across the ocean. Devin turned his kayak so it pointed straight to shore. "We need to go in right now!"

Cassie knew it. At least two of her blisters had popped, making her palms sting, but that didn't matter. They couldn't stay out on the water during a thunderstorm. Water conducted electricity, which meant if lightning struck anywhere even remotely close to them, they could all get hurt.

Paddling as fast as she could, she followed Devin and Hailey to land. She wasn't nearly as fast as they were, but Devin ran back into the water after getting Hailey out to grab Cassie's boat and pull her ashore.

Once she was out, they sprinted toward the street.

"Do you know anyone who lives here?" Devin shouted over the sound of the storm, gesturing at the big beach houses perched behind the dunes.

"Summer houses!" she yelled back. "There might not be anyone living in them right now."

"That porch is covered." He pointed toward the closest house. "Let's go!" He picked up Hailey and made a run for it.

Racing to keep up, Cassie had never been more thankful for her water shoes in her life. Her hands were cut up enough from the blisters; she didn't need any additional cuts or splinters on her feet.

On the porch, Devin set Hailey down. Cassie wiped the rain from her face, breathing hard from the run. Devin, meanwhile, didn't appear to have broken a sweat.

"Whew," Cassie wheezed, bending over and putting her hands on her knees. "I haven't had to run like that in a long time."

"I guess that's one of the benefits of needing to recertify as a lifeguard every two years," Devin said. "I can't afford not to stay in shape." Then his eyes went comically large. "Not that you're out of shape or anything," he added quickly.

Cassie laughed, her breath still coming in gasps. "Oh, no worries. I'm not offended."

Disappointed that they might not be on the same page about Tyler? Yes. But offended? No.

Devin gestured toward the door. "I'm gonna ring the bell."

"Wait. Let me catch my breath first."

She hadn't been out running since she brought Tyler home. Maybe she should get one of those jogging strollers and get back to it now that the weather was warming up.

But if she invested in a jogging stroller and then lost custody of Tyler, it would sit there collecting dust and depressing her every time she saw it. Better to wait and see what happened before making a big purchase like that.

The porch where they were taking cover was big enough for a couple of wicker chairs and an old-fashioned wooden porch swing. Hailey had already situated herself on the swing and was rocking back and forth. "We had to run a mile in gym class. They timed us. I did it in twelve minutes and twenty-nine seconds!"

"Good job, peanut," Devin said, ruffling her wet hair. Then he rang the doorbell. They all held their breath, the relentless pounding of the rain their only soundtrack.

But no one came to the door.

Devin glanced at Cassie. "Should we call someone?" They'd both made good use of their waterproof pouches.

She shook her head. "Let's wait until the rain dies down." Jonah couldn't come get them during school hours, but Alex would definitely make the trip as soon as they called, and it was probably overprotective of her, but she didn't want to send him out in the rain.

Lightning flashed and thunder cracked, making Hailey squeal. "I'm not scared," she announced, "just surprised! I used to be scared of lightning, but Daddy says it's like God's flashlight. He's shining it down on us from Heaven, saying hello."

Cassie smiled. "That's a nice sentiment." It surprised her a little that Devin could be so…poetic. But then again, she supposed he'd have been forced to develop at least a bit of whimsy to raise a little girl all on his own.

She wondered again about Hailey's mother. What would make a woman willingly walk away from her own child?

Hailey scrunched her nose. "What's a sentymen?"

"She said 'sentiment,' silly pants," Devin replied, chuckling. "It means a thought or a feeling."

"Oh. Okay. Can we play with my Lite-Brite when we get home?"

"Sure. That's a good idea."

"Do you want to play, Miss Cassie?"

"I need to dry off and pick up Tyler from my aunt's house."

"Tyler can play, too!"

"He's not big enough for Lite-Brite just yet. He'll try to eat the pieces."

Hailey grimaced. "Ew. Why?"

"Because babies will try to eat anything. Putting things in their mouth is part of how they learn about the world."

The little girl whipped her head toward her dad. "Did I do that?"

He nodded. "You especially liked to chew on your fist." He mimed biting his fingers.

Hailey looked down at her hand. "I did? That's so weird!"

"Yup, you were a weird one! Still are, if you ask me."

"Daddy!" She giggled. "You're weird!"

He reached out to tickle her, and she laughed harder. From a distance, the sound of a siren cut through the *plop-plop* of the rain.

Cassie closed her eyes and said a quick prayer—she always did when she heard a siren or saw the distinctive red-and-blue lights of an emergency vehicle. *God, please help whoever needs help right now. Help the first responders do their jobs quickly and well.*

But then a police car pulled up directly in front of the house where they were sitting, lights flashing.

She barely had time to toss Devin a confused look before the officer was exiting his car, hand on his service weapon.

"County sheriff!" he called out, his voice loud and hard. "Freeze! Stay right where you are!"

Devin couldn't believe this was happening. "Is this really necessary? My daughter's standing right there."

He'd already completed three field sobriety tests—following a penlight with his eyes, standing on one leg and doing a walk-and-turn test—and he was starting to get annoyed.

"Are you refusing to take the breathalyzer test?" the officer demanded. He'd pulled Devin off the porch, next to the patrol car, in the rain. The drops had slowed, but they hadn't stopped. The grizzled officer, who probably had fifteen or twenty years on Devin, didn't seem to care.

Devin threw his hands in the air. "We didn't even drive here!"

"Sir!" the officer yelled. "Calm! Down!"

Devin held his hands out in front of him. He needed to de-escalate this situation immediately. "I'm fine. I'm calm. I'll take the test. This is all just a big misunderstanding. I haven't been drinking or doing drugs."

The officer snorted, and Devin closed his eyes. Of course, the officer who'd booked him for his one and only DUI almost ten years ago was the one who'd responded to today's trespassing call. *Of course.*

The man must have a memory like an elephant, too, because it had been clear from the moment he saw him that he knew exactly who Devin was. And he'd obviously decided to make this whole thing as painful as possible.

That's what you get for being an idiot.

Devin tried not to beat himself up for mistakes he'd made in the past, but sometimes it was hard, especially in a small town like Sandpiper Cove. People here didn't forget. They *forgave*, mostly, but the past lingered in hushed voices and covert glances and moms who were nice to your face at school but wouldn't let their daughters come over to play.

What other people think of you is none of your business. Devin had learned a long time ago to focus on the things he could control—keeping his side of the street clean—rather than other people's opinions. At the moment, that meant practicing gratitude for the fact that he hadn't hurt anyone back when he was a reckless teen driving under the influence.

But the fact that Hailey had to see this…the fact that *Cassie* had to see this…it stung. Here he was trying to prove that he was a good guy, that she should trust him, and then this police officer—who would obviously never give him the benefit of the doubt—pulls up and tosses everything out the window.

Maybe she was right to keep her distance. Maybe he'd never be the man she needed him to be.

Demoralized, he blew into the breathalyzer machine, then waited a few seconds until the screen showed the officer what Devin knew it would show: Zero. Nada. Zip.

"Huh," the cop said.

Devin threw a glance over his shoulder at the porch. "Can we go home now?"

"Mrs. Murphy saw you on the feed from her doorbell camera, thought you were casing the joint."

Great. From drunk and disorderly to thievery. What other crimes could this guy invent to heap on Devin's shoulders? "Did she not see that we had a seven-year-old with us?"

"Good cover, bringing a kid along when you're getting ready to rob a place."

"She's not a cover—she's my daughter. A little girl who got caught out on the water during a thunderstorm."

The officer looked down his nose at Devin. "The penalty for trespassing in Massachusetts is up to thirty days in prison."

Devin's stomach pitched with incredulity. "Are you seriously going to arrest us?"

The officer sighed, glancing toward the porch, where Cassie and Hailey were anxiously waiting. "No. Go home. Check the weather report next time before you go out on the water with your kid."

The tension in Devin's body eased. "Thank you. I will."

"And you better stay out of trouble, Spencer," the cop warned him. "I've got my eye on you now. You mess up again and it will be my personal pleasure to put your sorry self in jail."

Chapter Eleven

"Well," Cassie said from her perch on Devin's front stoop, "I certainly wasn't expecting our outing to end like *that*."

It had been scary when the police officer had first confronted them, and scarier still when he'd taken Devin out into the rain to perform a sobriety check.

All the irritation she'd felt over his comment about Tyler's father had fled the moment Officer Keeland had pulled him off the porch, leaving only shocked concern in its wake.

Thankfully, the officer had been pleasant enough after the sobriety check: offering them a ride, letting Hailey play with the lights and siren, and giving the little girl a stuffed police bear. Hailey had named it Fuzzy, and she was now on her way to introduce him to all the other stuffed animals and dolls in her room.

"Does Hailey know that the police are sometimes called the fuzz?"

"Are they still called that?" Devin asked, looking slightly scandalized. "And no, she'd better not."

"I'm just glad he didn't arrest us."

"There weren't any 'no trespassing' signs posted around that house. We would have been fine." He paused. "Eventually."

"Still." Cassie shuddered. Her clothes were wet and cold. "Wouldn't have been fun to get hauled to the police station."

"Nope," Devin said flatly. "Not at all."

"What did he say to you out by the car?"

"Not much."

"Why was he so dead set on doing a sobriety test? We weren't even driving anywhere."

Devin scrubbed his hands over his eyes. "I've got history with that guy."

"History? What kind of history?" Cassie asked, confused.

Devin kicked a pebble off the side of the porch. "I need to get changed so I can go rescue the kayaks."

"Sure, but tell me what happened first."

He gave a long sigh. "Your aunt already knows about this. I didn't hide anything from her when she offered me the job."

Cassie's brow furrowed. This sounded bad. Very, very bad. "I never said you did."

"I know you didn't want to hire me because of who I was back then."

"Devin, we've talked about this. Eggshells, remember? It's in the past."

"Right." He shot her a skeptical look. His eyes, normally full of mischief, were wary. "Don't you need to go get Tyler?"

"Aunt Mirriam's dropping him off later. Just tell me."

"Fine." He blew out a breath. "I didn't stop partying when you went away to college, and I… I didn't always have someone I could count on to drive me home."

"Oh, Devin." Her heart fell. Not because she was angry, but because she was hurting on his behalf. "Tell me you didn't get arrested."

He scoffed and shook his head. "I wish I could."

"What happened?"

"My license was suspended. Had to pay a bunch of fines. Got sent to treatment classes."

"Did they help?"

"I was a seventeen-year-old kid with a chip on my shoulder. What do you think?"

Cassie bit her lip. From the way he was talking about it, she was pretty sure it hadn't helped one bit. "But no jail time?"

"No. Thank goodness. I qualified for the juvenile diversion program. And even though I didn't get sober for another three years or so, I at least smartened up to the fact that I couldn't drink and drive."

"Well, that was a blessing."

"Yep. God protected me there. And then later by giving me Hailey. I think He knew that I wouldn't get sober for myself."

She'd been to a handful of Al-Anon meetings back when she was still married, and based on some of the things she'd heard there, his statement set off alarm bells in her head. "When I was trying to get Jared to admit that he had a problem, people kept telling me he had to want it for himself, not for anyone else."

Devin hitched his shoulders. "Sometimes that's true. Sometimes it's not. Depends on the individual, I guess. Personally, I needed the outside reason. *Poor me, poor me, pour me a drink* is a saying in AA for a reason. The more I focused on myself and what I didn't have, the more entitled I felt to drink. Having Hailey gave me a purpose. Being her dad was more important to me than the selfish nonsense that was pushing me to drink."

Cassie mulled that over for a second. "You're a good dad."

He nodded. "Thanks."

"But what about when she grows up and doesn't need you anymore?"

"Kids always need their parents."

"But not as much, and not in the same way she needs you now."

Devin gazed up at the sky, and Cassie watched him closely. The rain had stopped now, although the cloud cover was still intact. Insects buzzed in the bushes. Birds chirped in the trees.

And in the distance, waves crashed to the shore. "Are you asking me if I'm afraid I'll go back to drinking?"

Cassie wasn't sure why she felt nervous waiting for his answer, but she did. "Are you?"

"How much do you know about the twelve steps?"

"A bit. I've been to a few Al-Anon meetings."

"Did you guys study the steps or read the Big Book?" The Big Book was the nickname given to the book that the founders of Alcoholics Anonymous had written back in the 1930s to explain what the twelve steps were and how to use them to recover from alcoholism.

She shook her head. "They were mostly discussion meetings. Not Big Book studies."

"And what did you discuss? Whatever was going on in your lives?"

"Pretty much, but in the context of the Three C's."

"And what are those?" he asked, although it was obvious he knew what they were and was leading her to say it out loud.

"You didn't cause it, you can't control it and you can't cure it."

"Right." He nodded. "It's the same thing for me. I can't control or cure my alcohol problem, but that's okay, because God can, and I've handed the whole thing over to Him. Those spiritual experiences they talk about in the Big Book, and in the Bible? They're real. God changed me, and now all my daily habits are built around supporting that change."

He caught her gaze and looked her straight in the eye. "So, no. I'm not afraid that when Hailey grows up, I'll go back to drinking. I'm different now—because of her, but more importantly, because of God and what He's done for me."

Goose bumps rose on Cassie's arms, and they weren't from the wind blowing against her damp clothes. It was his words. His confidence in his recovery, his faith in the Lord and his sure, strong words.

Maybe…maybe she'd been too hasty in turning down his dinner invitation. It would definitely be strange to start dating one of Jonah's friends, but as far as she could tell, she and Devin had been spending way more time together lately than he and Jonah. And three years wasn't an insurmountable age difference—it was unlikely that anyone would bat an eye.

No, from the moment he'd reentered her life as an adult, her main stumbling block had always been his history with alcohol. Getting burned so badly by Jared had made her wary of giving her attraction to him any fuel at all.

Because Jared hadn't changed, she'd assumed that Devin couldn't have changed, either. Or, if he had, that it was only a matter of time until he stumbled and fell back into his old ways.

But she'd been wrong.

People did change. God worked miracles in everyday lives. And some men chose to take accountability for their mistakes and put in the work to make sure they never made those same mistakes again while others simply…walked away.

A verse she loved, a verse she often relied on, sprang to mind: *My grace is sufficient for thee: for my strength is made perfect in weakness. Most gladly therefore will I rather glory in my infirmities, that the power of Christ may rest upon me.*

But then Devin's mouth quirked with mischief. "Of course, that's not to say I wouldn't love to extend my dad streak and give Hailey a brother or sister one day."

And just like that, Cassie knew that her refusal to go out to dinner with him had been the right call after all.

She'd never be able to help him give Hailey a biological brother or sister.

And given all the uncertainty around Tyler's future, she wasn't even sure she'd ultimately be able to adopt.

So she'd have to stuff her admiration of Devin and how far he'd come since they were teenagers back into a box.

Friends was the most the two of them could ever be.

* * *

The foster kids coming to Camp Piper that Saturday were all boys—most teenagers, but one just ten years old.

Since there were only twelve kids, they'd decided to split them into two groups: one would go kayaking with Devin and Cassie in the morning, while the other would play volleyball and learn survival skills with Jonah and Alex. In the afternoon, they'd switch groups, then feed the boys a campfire dinner before sending them back to Boston on the bus.

It was a pleasant day, around sixty degrees, and an array of wildflowers were out around the camp: daffodils, bluebells and a bunch of others Devin couldn't name. The cherry trees and crabapples were starting to bud, too, but their blossoms wouldn't make an appearance for another week or two.

The door to the minibus opened, and a large older man in khaki pants and a striped button-down emerged. "Morning, folks," he said, patting his comb-over. "I take it you're expecting us?"

"Yes, sir," Jonah said, stepping forward and proffering his hand. "I'm Jonah, and this is Devin, Alex and Cassie."

"Mark Corbett," the man said, shaking each of their hands in turn. "I told the boys to stay on the bus until you're ready for them."

Devin rubbed his hands together in anticipation. "We're ready." This was it—their trial run. If things went well today, they'd know they were in a good spot for the summer. If things didn't go well…well, he didn't want to think about that.

"I shared this with Mirriam, so she probably passed it along already, but there's a few things you should know."

"Best to hear it again and make sure everyone's on the same page," Jonah replied.

"They're good boys but they need a strong hand. Especially the older ones. Think they know it all, if you know what I mean."

Devin grinned. "I may or may not be able to relate to that."

"And I'm a PE teacher," Jonah added. "I'm used to dealing with teenage shenanigans."

"Excellent," Mark said. "And we have one kid who…well, Parker's very young."

"Is he the ten-year-old?" Cassie asked.

"Yes, and he just came to us a month ago. It's been a tough transition for him, especially since the other boys are older."

"Can I ask why he's with you?" Cassie said. "Why did they put such a young kid in residential care?"

"He's a special needs child. Can't walk. Sometimes it's hard to find the right placement when that's the case."

Alex frowned, squinting at the bus. "That's not right."

"Agreed," Mark said.

"Poor kid," Cassie murmured. Alex just kept staring at the bus.

"Well," Jonah said, clapping his hands. "We can have him help us ref the volleyball game, and Alex can probably do a special project with him, too. Maybe a little woodworking or some other kind of craft."

"Sounds good." Mark looked around. "You won't have any trouble navigating the wheelchair where you need it to go?"

"We're good," Jonah replied. "We've got a paved path to the dining hall, and the sports field is right next to it. Shouldn't be a problem."

"Great. I'll be here to help, of course, along with one of our aides." He called the boys off the bus, and Devin clocked how closely Alex watched the youngest boy as he exited the bus via the wheelchair lift, the aide right behind him.

"All right, fellas," Jonah called out, beckoning the boys to gather around him in a semicircle. "We're going to split you up into two groups today for some sports and kayaking. We'll start with a buffet lunch in the dining hall, and we'll end the day with a cookout at the campfires. Any questions?"

"Yeah," one of the older kids said, snickering. "Who's the babe?"

Devin's fists clenched as Jonah frowned. "The *babe*," Jonah said pointedly, waving in Cassie's direction, "is my sister. So show some respect."

"Nah, not her, man." The kid thrust his chin past Jonah. *"Her."*

When Devin turned to see who the boy was talking about, he just about swallowed his tongue in shock. There, standing in the parking lot of Camp Piper in stiletto heels, a tight pencil skirt and a crisp white blouse, was Shannon.

"Mommy!" Hailey gasped.

"Happy birthday, darling," she said to their daughter, smiling tightly, but her eyes never left Devin's face.

Chapter Twelve

After confirming with Jonah, Cassie and Alex that he could have a few minutes alone with Shannon, Devin promptly marched her from the parking lot to the pond, away from little pitchers with big ears. "Hailey's birthday was two weeks ago, Shannon."

"Well—" she held out her right hand to study her nails "—I'm here now. Did you want me to just ignore it?"

"I wanted you to reply to my texts two weeks ago. Pick up the phone and give your daughter a call."

She turned up her nose. "Nobody talks on the phone anymore. What is this? 2012?"

Seriously? "Shannon." Honestly, he didn't even know why he tried. Actually, scratch that. He tried for Hailey. Always for Hailey, no matter how much it felt like he was banging his head against a brick wall. "What are you even doing here?"

"I was in Boston, looking for a condo. Then I figured, why not come down here and see you?"

"And it didn't occur to you to call ahead?"

She pushed a strand of her highlighted hair behind her ear, frowning. "You want me to go? I'll go." Spinning on her heel, she turned toward the parking lot.

"No." He reached for her arm. "You're here now. Hailey's already seen you."

"Then stop giving me a hard time, Devin. When we talked

about what to do about the pregnancy, you said you'd take her—no strings, no pressure. I came here because I wanted to, but if you're going to give me grief, quite frankly, I'd rather leave."

"You're right." She wasn't, but whatever. He'd eat humble pie for Hailey's sake. "I'm sorry. You caught me by surprise."

"When did you move out here to Nowheresville?" she asked, looking around with a skeptical expression on her face. "I thought you lived in town. I just about died when the lady at the coffee shop said you'd moved to a cabin at a camp. You're not looking to renounce civilization and live as one of those mountain men survivalists, are you?"

"I work here now. Housing's included."

She sniffed. "Must be nice."

"When's your big move?"

"End of August."

"Did you find anything when you were house hunting?"

"Yeah, a couple places." She was moving to Boston for a new job as the head of public relations at one of the big research hospitals. "They're expensive, but my father said he'd cover my down payment as long as I can handle the monthly mortgage payment on my own."

Devin bit his tongue to avoid throwing her words—*must be nice*—back in her face. Her father had always pampered her, and part of why she hadn't wanted to play any real role in their daughter's life was because she didn't want her dad to find out about Hailey and withdraw his financial support.

"So, I'm staying in this fab hotel in Hyannis tonight. Can Hailey come for a sleepover? I've already made an appointment for us to get mani-pedis at the hotel spa, and I'm pretty sure I can get her in for a cut and color, too."

"A cut's fine, but she's only seven. I don't want you coloring her hair." And as for the sleepover? He wasn't thrilled about the idea, but it might be a nice way for Hailey to spend some quality time with her mom.

Shannon pressed her hands together in supplication. "But we'd look so cute with matching highlights."

"No." Devin shook his head. "That's not appropriate for a little girl."

She pouted. "You're no fun anymore."

"Well, I'd rather be sober and boring than in debt, dead or in jail, which was the direction I was heading."

She scoffed at that. "Always so dramatic. You act like everyone else at college wasn't doing the exact same things we were."

"How many other college kids do you know who got married after a night of underage drinking?"

She shrugged. "We're not the first people to do something stupid in Vegas."

"Maybe not, but I can't afford to be stupid anymore. Hailey needs me. And that's not who God's calling me to be."

She rolled her eyes. "Right. Because God talks to you now."

"He was always right there with me. I just wasn't open to hearing Him before."

She gave his arm a condescending pat. "You do you, Dev. Just don't be surprised when people think you're a little—" she tapped her temple "—odd."

He shrugged. "I can live with that." He could, too. When he'd given up alcohol and stepped up to become a dad, he'd learned pretty quickly who was a real friend and who'd just been along for the ride.

The people who mattered to him didn't think his faith was odd. They were right next to him at his Celebrate Recovery meetings, right next to him at church. Some of them worked here at the camp with him. And one of them lived right next door.

He and Shannon quickly hashed out the details of the sleepover, and then he went to pack Hailey an overnight bag.

"But Daddy," Hailey whined as Devin grabbed her pajamas, "I wanted to kayak with the big boys!"

"You'll have lots of opportunities to kayak again at camp this summer. Don't you want to spend time with your mom?"

"Can't she come back tomorrow?"

He shook his head. "No, peanut. She has to fly back home to Colorado tomorrow. She came all this way to see you today."

Hailey tugged at the French braid Cassie had given her this morning, thinking it over. "I guess it's okay."

"You'll have fun. You'll get to sleep at the hotel with her."

That perked her up. "Will she let me watch a movie?"

"Probably. You can ask her."

"Okay!"

After that, she bounced outside and asked Shannon if she could watch a movie at the hotel. Shannon, smartly, said yes, and Hailey happily followed her to her rental car.

Devin knelt down and gave his daughter a hug before she got in the car. "If you change your mind and want to come home early, tell your mommy to call me."

"We're going to have the best time, aren't we, Hailey?" Shannon replied brightly.

"You know how to reach me if you need me," Devin told her.

Shannon tossed her hair over her shoulder. "Don't worry. We won't."

Devin watched them pull out of the parking lot. This was a good thing, wasn't it? Girls needed their moms, and Hailey hadn't even seen Shannon in person in more than a year.

So what if she was spoiled and a little immature? It wasn't Shannon who'd been hassled by a police officer right in front of Hailey's eyes just a few days ago.

Cassie came over and touched Devin's forearm. "Are you

ready for kayaking? Our group's done with lunch and watching the volleyball game at the moment, but they're getting antsy."

Devin shook off his worry and gave her a brisk nod. "Yeah, let's hit it."

Hailey, he had to believe, would be just fine.

Cassie moved her perfectly browned marshmallow away from the crackling campfire, grabbed two graham crackers and a big piece of chocolate, smooshed everything together into a s'more and took a bite. Ooey, gooey, warm and delicious.

And definitely a hit with the boys.

Overall, the day had gone incredibly well. Devin had been a bit distracted, but she couldn't blame him after the stunt his ex had pulled, and the boys had all had fun. They'd splashed each other kayaking, competed hard at volleyball and learned a few survival skills from Jonah, who'd taken them into the forest with a compass for a short hike. After that, they'd shown up for dinner around the campfire exhausted. Like teenage boys everywhere, though, the food had given them a strong second wind.

Even Parker, the young boy in a wheelchair, had had a good day. Alex had stuck close to his side, encouraging him, joking with him and helping him when he needed help.

Cassie glanced at Devin, who was staring into the fire. "Want me to make you a s'more?" she asked, plunking herself down beside him and elbowing him in the side.

"I'm good. Thanks, though."

"Any updates from Shannon?" The fire was a big one, with a column of smoke that wavered in the breeze. Cassie would have to wash her hair before going to bed tonight if she didn't want her bedding to smell like a campfire for days.

He pulled his phone out of his back pocket to show her a photo of Hailey getting her toenails painted at the spa.

"Aww. Looks like she's having fun."

"She's never had a sleepover before."

"Really? Never? I used to sleep over at friends' houses all the time."

"It's not something she's ever expressed interest in, and I'm grateful. In this day and age, you can't be too careful." One of the logs broke in two, sending sparks into the air.

"That's true, but she seemed excited about staying at the hotel."

"That's not something she's ever done, either."

Cassie's brows shot up. "You've never taken her on vacation?"

"We've visited my mom in Florida a couple of times, but we stayed at her place. I've never been in a position where I could afford a hotel."

Cassie thought about all the fancy trips she and Jared had taken—beautiful places, all of them, but those happy memories had been tainted when her ex-husband had finally revealed who he really was.

"Oh, well," she said, "you didn't miss out on much."

"No?"

"It's not the place that matters, it's the people you're with."

Shooting her an intense look that she felt from the ends of her hair to the tips of her toes, he nodded and opened his mouth to reply, but just then two of the kids started yelling.

Devin and Jonah both jumped to their feet.

"Take it back, Damien!" One of the teens shoved the other one hard in the chest. "I'm no simp!"

Damien stumbled back, caught his footing and lunged forward, grabbing his aggressor's shirt. "She's never gonna like you, Eli. You think you're so cool but you're a loser!"

"Hey!" Jonah grabbed Damien's upper arm. "Knock it off."

"I'm *not* a loser!" Eli yelled, red in the face. Devin, meanwhile, got right in between the two boys.

"You're poor, you're ugly, you're stupi—"

Eli swung at Damien, only missing because Devin threw his arm up and blocked the punch. “Enough!” Devin yelled. “Both of you! There’s a fire *right there*.”

Mark Corbett, who’d stepped away to make a phone call, came rushing back. “Damien! Eli! On the bus now!” He marched both boys away from the fire and off toward the parking lot.

The other kids looked at each other, not sure what to make of what had just happened. Parker, the ten-year-old, started to cry. Cassie rushed over to him.

“Hey, buddy, it’s okay. Nobody got hurt.”

The boy hid his face in his elbow. “Everybody’s always so mean to each other.”

“I’m sorry, honey.” Cassie patted his back.

Alex sat next to them, leaning his cane on a nearby log. “Are they mean to you, Parker?”

The boy sniffled. “Sometimes.”

Alex clenched his jaw. “What about the kids at school?”

“They’re not mean, but they make fun of me because I can’t read very well. The teacher already told me I don’t get to go to fifth grade next year. I have to stay in fourth. Like a baby.”

“You know what?” Alex confided. “I was a year behind in school, too.”

Parker’s mouth fell open in surprise. “You were?”

“My parents held me back from kindergarten so I could learn how to walk.”

“You couldn’t walk, either?”

Alex shook his head. “No, I have cerebral palsy. That’s why I limp and walk with a cane. But you know what having a disability’s taught me? Grit.”

“Like…dirt?”

Alex laughed. “No. When it comes to people, grit means determination and courage. The ability to stick with something and see it through even when it’s hard.”

"Oh."

Alex ruffled the boy's hair. "You can do it, buddy. I know everything feels scary and hard right now, but I believe in you."

Parker sniffled. "You're nice. Like my grandma used to be."

"I'm sorry you lost her," Alex said.

"Oh, I didn't lose her. She died."

"I know. And I'm sorry."

"Me, too," Cassie said. She and Alex exchanged a look over the boy's head. She felt for this kid. She really did. The thought of Parker, who was only a little bit older than Hailey, going back to a group home where the other kids were mean to him hurt her heart.

If she had to give up Tyler, then maybe…

"All right, everybody!" Jonah called out. "Put your marshmallow sticks in a pile over here, and then we'll head back to the bus."

"Boo!" one of the kids called out, giving Jonah a thumbs-down.

Devin laughed. "We had a great day with you, too. We'll talk to Mark and see if we can get you guys back out here soon."

Parker looked up at her and Alex, hope in his eyes.

It simultaneously crushed and uplifted her that one short conversation could inspire that kind of trust from a child.

This boy deserved a family, the same way Tyler deserved a family. The same way *she* deserved a family.

The reality in this life, though, was that people didn't always get what they deserved.

Chapter Thirteen

Devin was brushing his teeth when his phone rang, the name of Shannon's hotel in Hyannis displaying on the screen.

He rinsed out his mouth and swiped to answer the call. "Hey, Shannon." Honestly, he wasn't surprised she was calling. As he'd told Cassie, Hailey had never spent a night away from him in her life. He was tired from the day but glad he'd have a chance to wish his daughter sweet dreams.

"Daddy?" Hailey's voice wavered.

"What's up, peanut? Calling to say good night?"

"Daddy, I'm scared."

"What are you scared of? I know the hotel's a little different from home, but your mom's there to help you. There's nothing to be scared of."

"No, Daddy." Her little voice wobbled again. "Mommy left. She said she'd be back soon, but it's been forever. There's weird noises. I'm scared."

"What?" His tiredness was gone in a flash. "She's not there?"

"No."

"Are you sure? Maybe she's in the bathroom."

"She left, Daddy. She said she needed to go downstairs and she'd be back soon, but she's not back and I'm scared."

"What time did she leave?" He was really hoping Hailey would say something like *five minutes ago*. Maybe Shannon had run downstairs to pick up a toothbrush from the front desk, or some extra towels. Five minutes could feel like forever to a little girl who'd never spent the night away from home.

"I don't know." Devin could hear that she was holding back tears.

"Okay, sweetheart. Stay on the phone. I'm going to try calling her cell, but I'll come right back when I'm done."

"Okay," she whispered.

He put Hailey on hold and quickly dialed Shannon. It rang once, twice…and then went to voicemail. He growled in frustration. She'd pressed "ignore" on his call!

He called her again. Same result. And then again. And again.

What was she doing that she couldn't take his call?

He shot off a text: Call me right now.

Tapping his toe, he waited a full thirty seconds. Nothing. No call.

He clicked back over to Hailey. "Peanut? You okay?"

"Mm-hmm," she said, but it came out sounding watery.

"I'm going to come and pick you up, but it's going to take me about half an hour to get there. Do you know your room number?"

"No." Argh, why hadn't he asked Shannon to share the room number?

Because you never dreamed she'd leave Hailey there alone.

At least he knew which hotel they were in. And hopefully Shannon would call him back before he got there.

"Do you know which floor you're on?"

"The top floor," she said. "We went up in the elevator."

"Okay, sweetheart, that's good. I'll come find you." He didn't want to get off the phone, but he didn't have Bluetooth, so he had to hang up so he could drive. He tried calling Shannon again as he ran out to his truck, but no dice.

Where was she? Why wasn't she picking up?

Hailey's safe, she's fine, she's locked in the hotel room. No one's going to hurt her.

But he absolutely hated the thought of her being there all alone and scared.

He jammed his key into his ignition and…nothing.

Not now, stupid truck.

He tried again—"Come on"—but the engine still wouldn't turn over. "No!" He tried several more times in quick succession, then slammed the heel of his hand into the steering wheel.

The blare of his horn sounded into the night.

He hopped down from the truck and paced. What should he do? Order a rideshare? He checked the app. It would take almost twenty minutes for a car to even get here to pick him up.

He called Shannon again. Voicemail.

If she thought he'd ever give her another chance to spend time with their daughter on her own after this little stunt, she was sorely mistaken.

But what in the world was he going to do now?

Cassie's porch light was on. Maybe she'd lend him her car. He knocked quietly, hoping the sound wouldn't wake the baby.

She opened the door quickly, Tyler in her arms. "Everything okay?" she asked. "We heard your horn."

"Shannon left Hailey alone at the hotel, and my truck won't start. Can I borrow your car?"

"Are you kidding me? Yes, of course. Give me one sec to throw on some shoes. I'll drive." She held Tyler out to him and Devin took him. The baby patted him on the cheek.

"You don't need to put him to bed?"

She sighed as she reached for her running shoes. "He wasn't sleeping anyway. Sometimes taking him for a drive actually helps knock him out."

He nodded. Fair enough. "I hope the horn didn't wake him."

"Nope. Apparently he napped for *four hours* at Aunt Miriam's. He's not tired at all."

"Wow, dude. Four hours? Legend."

Cassie shoved her left foot into her shoe and quickly tied her laces. "Why did Shannon leave Hailey alone at the hotel?"

"I don't know. I've been calling and calling, but she won't pick up her cell."

"That's crazy. I hope she's okay."

"I always knew she was flaky, but this? This takes the cake."

Cassie finished tying her right shoe and stood. "Come on. Let's go."

He carried Tyler out to her car, then let her buckle the baby into his car seat. He protested for a split second, but she handed him a squeaky giraffe, and he immediately started gnawing on it.

When Cassie was clipped into the driver's seat, she asked, "Where are we headed?"

"Hyannis. The Cape Cod Grand."

She whistled. "Fancy."

"I never should have let Shannon take her for the night. Why did I think everything would go smoothly? I know her. She never follows through."

"Don't be so hard on yourself. No one would expect a mother to abandon her daughter in a strange hotel."

"I'm going to call Hailey back while you drive."

"Good idea."

He got the hotel on the line and asked the desk clerk to connect him to Shannon's room. Hailey didn't pick up, and Devin's imagination immediately went to a terrible place.

"She's not answering."

Cassie flicked a glance at him. "Maybe she's watching a movie."

Even that thought didn't comfort him. There was so much scary and inappropriate junk on TV these days, and if Hailey was alone in the room, that meant she had unfettered access to all of it.

He wished he was driving. He wished he had control over the speed of this car. "Can you go any faster?" he asked, his voice coming out choked.

"Devin." She flashed him a scolding look. "Tyler's in the car."

He knocked the back of his head against his seat. "Right. Sorry." Despite his haste to get to Hailey, he didn't want to put Cassie or the baby in danger.

But, man, it was hard to be this far away from his little girl when he didn't know if she was safe.

He tried calling Hailey again, but the phone just rang and rang. And when he called Shannon, it would ring once or twice before sending him to voicemail. It was going to take Herculean effort not to yell at her the moment he saw her.

When they reached the hotel, he leaped out in the driveway, while Cassie went to go park the car. He stormed into the lobby and straight to the elevators at the back. Thank goodness the clerk on the phone had given him Hailey's room number. If he'd been forced to wait in line at the check-in desk to get it, he'd probably have gotten into a fistfight trying to cut to the front.

The elevator was taking too long, so Devin found the back stairwell and bounded to the top level, taking the stairs two at a time. He raced into the hallway, scanning the room numbers for the one Hailey was in.

When he found it, he forced himself to calm down and knocked gently. "Hailey?" he called through the door. "It's Dad."

"Daddy?" she said, hiccupping.

"Open the door, peanut."

He heard her little footsteps pad toward him, then some scuffling as she tried to open the door.

"It won't open, Daddy!" she said, sounding panicked.

"Try again, honey. Twist the lock and then pull the door. If you can get it cracked, Dad will do the rest."

"I can't! The lock won't move!"

"Did you try turning it to the left?"

"Yes!"

"Okay, try turning it to the right."

"Oh."

"Did it move?"

"Yes."

"Good job. Now twist the handle and open the door."

There were a couple more thumps and bumps before she said, "The door's too heavy, Daddy."

"You're strong. You can do it. Pull harder." Meanwhile, he was wondering how long it would take to get one of the clerks up here to open it for them.

Finally, with a shout of triumph, she pulled the door back half an inch. Devin shot his hand out to push it all the way open.

Hailey flung herself at him, latching onto his waist like a little koala. "Daddy, Daddy, I was so scared!"

"I know, honey. I was, too," he said, lifting her all the way into his arms so she could wrap hers around his neck. "But I'm here now and everything's fine."

Which was all true, but it didn't mean he wasn't still livid with Shannon.

His anger could wait, though.

His daughter needed him, and that trumped anything and everything else.

Tyler had not fallen asleep in his car seat, so Cassie unbuckled him and took him into the lobby of the hotel. The Cape Cod Grand was a beautiful, old-timey resort with a sweeping front staircase, red carpets and a big chandelier. Cassie had only been here once, for the rehearsal dinner before her wedding, which Jared's family had hosted in the steakhouse on the main floor.

The food, predictably, had been delicious. Jared's parents had spared no expense on the rehearsal dinner, and the steak and lobster tail had probably been the best meal Cassie had ever eaten in her life. She wasn't surprised that Devin's stylish ex-wife was staying here. Who showed up at a summer camp in stilettos? Or left her daughter unattended in a hotel room?

Lord, help me stop being so judgmental.

Maybe the woman was injured.

That was literally the only thing Cassie could think of that would make this situation make sense.

Or maybe she still has a drinking problem and she's tying one on in the hotel bar.

She glanced around the lobby. She hadn't seen Devin yet, which she hoped meant that he'd found Hailey's room. Should she peek into the bar?

She hadn't expected to be asking herself that question ever again, but at least this time she wouldn't be going in there with a sense of dread hanging over her. It was much easier to be dispassionate when you were looking for a stranger rather than your spouse.

Tyler squawked in her arms, and she rubbed his back. She was shocked he hadn't fallen asleep in the car, but hopefully that meant he'd go straight to sleep when they started driving home.

If she and Jared had been able to start a family together, this might have been her life: walking into strange bars with a baby on her hip, hoping to find her husband and drag him back home before he'd had time to do too much damage to his wallet, his life or their marriage.

But if they'd been able to have a family, would his drinking have escalated the way it had at the end? He'd claimed it wouldn't have, but who knew? Like Devin had said the other day, he might simply have found some other excuse.

She supposed that saying she'd heard at Al-Anon was true after all: *Rejection is divine protection.*

But if God had rejected her request to start a family with Jared to protect her from him, who would He be protecting if He took Tyler away?

She bounced the baby in her arms. Enough wallowing. Devin and Hailey needed her support.

She poked her head into the bar. Sure enough, there was Shannon, laughing at something the man next to her was saying, her legs crossed and a martini glass in her hand. Should Cassie go in there and say something to her? She wanted to, strangely, but it certainly wasn't her place.

She pulled her phone out of her back pocket and texted Devin: Did you find Hailey? Is everything okay?

He replied quickly. Yes and yes. On our way downstairs.

Relief had her stepping out of the bar so she could meet them in the lobby. She couldn't wait to give Hailey a great big hug.

Devin stepped off the elevator with Hailey in his arms. Cassie raised her left hand and waved, since she had Tyler on her right hip.

"Miss Cassie!" Hailey said, her face lighting up. "You're here, too!"

"We're here, honey, and we're so glad you're okay."

Hailey leaned over and wrapped her arms around Cassie's neck. Cassie and Devin somehow managed to switch children without losing their balance or dropping anyone, and Cassie hugged Hailey back, breathing in the sweet scent of her little-girl shampoo.

"My mom left me," Hailey whispered, her grip on Cassie tightening.

"I know. That wasn't nice of her."

"I thought I was stuck, but Daddy helped me open the door to get out."

"Your dad's pretty cool, isn't he?"

Hailey nodded. "I'm tired. Can we go home?"

Devin and Cassie traded glances, Cassie motioning toward the bar with a tilt of her head. "Your dad might want to say goodbye to your mom, let her know where you're going."

"Okay," Hailey said, sounding sleepy.

"I can take her to the car if you want to go talk to Shannon."

"You don't mind?"

She shook her head. "As long as you don't mind hanging onto Tyler."

"Nope. Tyler's my bud. And he might keep me from saying something I'll regret."

Cassie got it. The weight of a child, the sweetness of a baby—they were good at taking the edge off. And Devin had certainly been edgy on the drive here. "Take your time. We'll be in the car."

Hailey wasn't light, but carrying her outside to the car and sitting with her while she fell asleep was a straight-up privilege.

Chapter Fourteen

"Shannon." Devin wasn't sure how he managed to keep his voice level, but he did.

The bar was dark and plush, the kind of place that sold expensive cocktails. In other words, the exact opposite of the frat parties and cheap Irish pubs he and Shannon used to frequent in college.

It felt like a lifetime ago that he'd been that stupid kid, always on the hunt for a good time. He hadn't realized back then that responsibility and purpose would make him feel a million times better than partying ever had.

Shannon, clearly, had not come to the same conclusion.

She took her hand off the arm of the man she was talking to and beamed at him. It was obvious that she was feeling no pain. "Devin, Devin, Devin. Fancy meeting you here."

"You left our daughter alone in a strange hotel to come down here and have a drink?"

She waved her hand dismissively. "She's fine. The door's locked. I checked."

He gritted his teeth and asked God for help to stay calm. "She's seven. She's not fine. She was scared."

"I just came down for a quick minute to talk to my new friend Anton here." She gave a finger-wave to the man sitting next to her, who now looked distinctly uncomfortable. "I've hardly been gone at all."

"You've been gone for almost an hour! I had time to drive all the way here from Sandpiper Cove!"

The man Shannon had been talking to got to his feet and slid a few bills onto the bar. "Let me just get out of your way…"

Shannon reached out and grabbed his wrist before he could walk off. "Don't go. Devin was just leaving."

Unbelievable. Devin shook his head, disgusted. "You put our daughter in danger, Shannon, and you don't even seem to care."

"She was *fine*. You didn't have to come down here, all knight-in-shining-armor. She was in bed watching a movie, happy as a clam. We had a great afternoon."

"She called me and begged me to come because *you wouldn't pick up your phone.*"

Shannon took a long sip of her martini with her free hand. "I told her I'd be back before the movie was over. You can't expect me to be at her beck and call twenty-four-seven."

Devin gaped at her. "You're the one who asked for the sleepover. And now you're telling me that one night is too much for you?"

Anton quietly dislodged his wrist from Shannon's grasp and slinked away. At the same time, Tyler took his hand out of his mouth and shoved his wet fingers in Devin's ear. "Eww, dude." Devin moved the little guy's hand away.

"Devin," Shannon said, her mouth forming a surprised O as she noticed the baby for the first time. "Don't tell me you had another baby?"

"No, he's not mine."

"But where did he come from?" she asked, seeming absolutely astonished.

"Tyler's not the issue right now."

"You're literally the only man I've ever met who actually wants kids."

What was she talking about? "There's lots of guys who want families."

"Nuh-uh, nuh-uh." She shook her head in an exaggerated way, reminding him that she definitely wasn't sober. "Nobody our age wants kids. You're like a weird throwback to the 1950s or something."

"You're drunk. Go get some sleep. We can talk about this in the morning."

She visibly deflated. "I never wanted to be a mom, you know."

He sighed. "I know. But it happened. And if you want to spend time with your daughter, you can't leave her alone to go drinking at the hotel bar."

"I thought maybe I could be like a cool aunt rather than a mother, but it's just so *boring*. How have you done this every day for the last six years?"

"Seven," he corrected her, feeling his hackles rising again. Boring? Hailey? It was so far from the truth it was laughable.

"When I move to Boston, I'll hire a nanny. That way, I can spend time with her without being bored out of my mind."

"If it's such a chore, you don't have to spend any time with her." In fact, after this, it would almost certainly be better if she didn't.

"I want to. Really. And you're the one who's always trying to get me to visit and call."

"Well, we're done with that now. If you want to see her, you reach out to me. But no more sleepovers. And no babysitters. I'm not sending her to Boston so you can ignore her and hand her off to someone else. And if you ever have another drink while you're supposed to be watching her..." he said, his jaw tightening, "that's the end of it. I won't let you see her again."

Shannon took another sip of her drink, watching him over the rim of her glass. "You're hilarious when you're mad."

He spun on his heel. "Good night, Shannon."

She laughed. "If I want to spend time with her, I'll spend time with her. All I have to do is snap my fingers and my father's lawyers will be all over you."

Devin kept walking, refusing to dignify her statement with a response.

She hadn't wanted to tell her father about the pregnancy or the birth of their daughter, and Devin had been more than happy to go along with her wishes on that. If she ever changed her mind, though, and brought him into the loop… Devin had no doubt that her statement would be nothing but the truth.

When Devin came out to the car, he quietly buckled Tyler into his car seat. Cassie eased out of the back seat, where she'd been sitting with her arm around a sleeping Hailey. "Everything okay?" she whispered, stretching her legs as she stood.

Standing next to her little Chevy, he leaned forward and placed his forehead on the roof. "No," he replied, his voice muffled. "Not really."

"What happened?"

"She was right where you said she'd be. Drinking."

"Ugh." Cassie shook her head. Leaving a little girl alone to go to the bar? It wasn't right. "What did she have to say for herself?"

"Nothing good. She thought I was overreacting and Hailey was fine."

"Why wasn't she answering her phone?"

He still had his forehead on the roof of the car, and she walked over to him, concerned by the fact that he sounded so defeated. "Who knows? Because she was flirting with some guy, probably. But she said I couldn't expect her to be at Hailey's beck and call twenty-four-seven."

Cassie's mouth dropped open. "She said that? Really? After she asked to take Hailey on a sleepover?"

"That's exactly what I said!" he exclaimed, lifting his head.

"She's got some nerve, doesn't she?" Cassie had half a mind to march right back into the hotel bar and give Shannon a piece of her mind.

"You can say that again. Her dad's rich, and he brought her up as a total pampered princess."

"Good thing she doesn't live on Cape Cod."

"Yeah, but now that she's moving to Boston..."

Cassie made a face. "You think she's going to want to see Hailey more?"

"I know she will. She just told me."

The parking lot was well-lit but mostly empty. From behind the hotel, she could hear the muted burble of the ocean. A car drove past on the road out front, momentarily illuminating them both in the glow of its headlights. Devin's gray eyes looked dark and inky in the night, and Cassie felt locked into his gaze, like she couldn't look away.

He was a good man, a good father—he shouldn't have to deal with ridiculousness like this. "Can you get your lawyer to amend whatever visitation rights she has in your custody agreement? Based on what happened tonight, it shouldn't be too hard, should it?"

Devin closed his eyes, unease sinking deep into the lines of his face. "I don't have a lawyer, Cass. We've never had a formal custody agreement."

That certainly complicated things. She reached out to pat his shoulder in reassurance. "You know what they say. The best time to plant a tree was twenty years ago. The second-best time is today."

"Thanks to living at camp, at least now I have the money for a lawyer. Or a consultation, at least."

She moved her hand from his shoulder to his forearm, giving him an encouraging squeeze. "There you go. Call around tomorrow. From what I understand, most of them will do a discovery call for free."

He nodded, then covered her hand with his own, and she had to suppress a shiver. Did he feel it, too, the pull between them? "Thanks for driving us out here."

"Of course."

"It probably feels like a flashback to high school, doesn't it? You having to drive me around in the middle of the night." They were standing close, very close, and his voice was low and edged with gravel.

"It's nothing like high school, Devin," she said, and it wasn't. Tonight, she wasn't driving around a reckless kid with no sense of self-preservation; she was driving a father who'd do anything to protect his child.

"I had the biggest crush on you back then."

A shimmer of surprise and delight shot through her. "You did?"

He nodded, tilting his head. "Big-time. But you were too good for me. Older, smarter. I was such a mess, and you were always so put together."

It was funny to her that that's how he'd seen her. She'd felt like a big dork in high school. *Responsible Cassie, reliable Cassie. Washed-up, boring, infertile Cassie.*

Or maybe she hadn't felt like that in high school—maybe that's how she'd come to see herself by the end of her time with Jared.

"You don't think I was kind of…boring?"

His brow furrowed in confusion. "You're the exact opposite of boring."

Another flicker of delight unfurled inside her, even as she tried to discredit what he'd said. "You don't know me that well."

He didn't let her get away with that. "I've known you for more than twenty years, and with all the time we've spent together lately, I'd say I know you extremely well." He looked right into her eyes as he said the next part: "You, Cassandra Reed, are the most fascinating person I've ever met."

Of its own accord, her body swayed toward him. Suddenly, he had one firm, strong hand at the small of her back and the other on the side of her face. "I'm going to kiss you now," he said, his eyes searching, his hand gently cupping the soft skin of her cheek.

She didn't move, didn't breathe.

He dipped his head, his lips barely brushing hers, and that flicker of delight turned into an inferno.

She made a sound in the back of her throat, and his mouth came back to hers, staunch and steadfast, steady and true.

Another car drove by, lighting them up, and Devin stepped away. "Wow," he said, looking stunned.

Cassie knew the feeling. She couldn't remember a kiss ever, *ever*, making her feel like that, and it terrified her. She'd always known Devin would be trouble, but still, she'd done a horrible job of guarding her heart.

"You'll go out to dinner with me now, won't you?"

She wanted to—badly—but the reason things hadn't worked out with Jared would stand in the way with Devin, too. *Trouble, trouble, trouble.* She forced herself to shake her head.

"It's not a good idea, Dev. I got caught up in the moment, but…we need to think about what's best for the camp, and for the kids." She squinted at the dark windows of the car. Tyler hadn't made a peep since Devin had deposited him in his car seat, and she hoped that meant the baby had finally gone to sleep, the same as Hailey.

Hurt rubbed at the edges of his voice. "I wish you'd think less about everything and everyone else and more about what *you* want for once."

She was thinking of herself, though—and how much it would hurt to let herself walk farther down this road with him only to find herself, once again, at a total dead end.

Chapter Fifteen

Under the direction of Walter Worthington, the geriatric DJ Alex had hired for the family dance at Camp Piper's open house, Devin and Jonah were hanging a disco ball in the dining hall.

Jonah was keeping the ladder steady while Devin was up top, holding the disco ball so that Walter could see if the placement looked right before Devin drilled a ceiling hook into the beam overhead.

"That's right, boys, right there'll be perfect," Walter said. He was an older gentleman with bushy white eyebrows and a brown corduroy cap that matched his brown corduroy pants. Apparently, he was one of the residents at the senior living community where Alex worked. Devin had his doubts about the man's DJing prowess, but Cassie and Jonah had both seemed happy with Alex's recommendation, so Devin had kept his mouth shut.

So what if the guy ended up playing a bunch of oldies? The teenagers at the dance might snicker, but the little kids wouldn't know any better. The point of the dance wasn't to throw the world's best party—it was to get people onsite so they could see Camp Piper's charm.

"Great," Devin called down, marking the spot where he was going to drill with a pencil. Once that was done, he made his way down the ladder to exchange the disco ball for the drill.

"You're going to clear the tables out of here for the dance, yes?" Walter asked.

Devin and Jonah exchanged a glance. "We'll push them to the sides to make a dance floor, but we're serving food outside and people will want to sit down."

"Hmm," Walter said, stroking his chin. "And how many folks are you expecting?"

"I don't know," Devin said, looking to Jonah. "Did we decide to use that online ticketing app?"

"We did," his friend confirmed, "and so far we've got about fifty people signed up."

Devin's heart sank. The dance was coming up quickly, and that was nowhere near the kind of crowd they were hoping for. "That's it?"

Jonah shot him a pained look. "People might be waiting until the last minute to decide. Or they saw the details on the flyer but didn't bother to go online and reserve a spot."

Devin rubbed his temples. "And how about registration for summer camp? Any takers there?"

"A few," Jonah said, keeping it vague.

"A few as in…three? Thirty? Ballpark it for me."

"More than three, less than thirty."

Devin winced. To make a real go of this camp thing, they needed more like three *hundred* campers this summer. "I have a lot riding on this, Jonah. What else can we do to get people signed up?"

"I mean, we're doing it, Dev. We've got flyers up all over Cape Cod, we spoke at that school last week—"

"*One* school. Can't we get into any others?"

"Alex has been calling, but it's closing in on the end of the year. Things get busy, and they don't have time to fit us in."

"What about your high school?"

Jonah shook his head. "The principal said no."

If they couldn't even get the principal of Jonah's school to agree to let them come give a talk, they were in trouble.

"Boys," Walter said, adjusting his cap. "Come give a talk about your camp at the retirement community. We love having outside speakers there."

"No offense," Devin said, "but you're not really our target audience, Walter."

The older man lifted one of his bushy eyebrows. "Ah, so you're planning to ignore all those grandparents with disposable income to spend on their grandchildren because…?"

Devin and Jonah exchanged another look. For some reason, Devin had assumed that Alex's retirement community was for seniors on a fixed income. But if that wasn't the case… "You really think they'd be interested in hearing about what we do here?"

"Why not? Like I said, we always enjoy having outside speakers. And if you invite us all to your dance, I'm guessing a bunch of us will bring our kids and grandkids with us, as well."

"Walter," Jonah said slowly. "That sounds like a great idea."

The older man beamed. "Fantastic. Give the office a call when you're done hanging the disco ball. They'll get you penciled in." He said goodbye, and Devin and Jonah went back to work.

Once the disco ball was up, the two of them stood back and admired its flash and shine. "Well," Jonah said, hands on his hips, "I never thought we'd be trying to give the dining hall a nightclub flavor."

"The campers'll like it. If we manage to get anyone signed up, that is."

"Have a little faith, my man," Jonah said, squeezing his shoulder as he steered him out of the dining hall and into the sunshine.

Devin squinted against the light. "Easy for you to say. If this doesn't work out, you still have your job at the high school."

Devin had actually heard from several of his former colleagues at the country club that things with Lucas might not be working out as well as the owner had hoped. It might not hurt to give Charles a call to check in about the status of his old job.

"How'd it go the other day with Shannon?" Jonah asked. "Cass said she had to drive you to Hyannis in the middle of the night to pick up Hailey?"

"Yeah, she did. And it went about as well as anything with Shannon ever goes."

"So not good, then?"

Devin shook his head. "No."

"Sorry, man."

"I've had consult calls with a couple of lawyers about how to start getting a formal custody plan in place."

"Sounds smart."

Devin rubbed the back of his neck. "I don't know. I'm leery of pulling the trigger. Her dad's loaded, and if she decides to get him involved, his legal team could probably work it so that she ends up with primary custody and I only get her every second Sunday."

Jonah frowned. "Seems unlikely."

"What Shannon wants, Shannon tends to get."

"But she's never wanted much to do with Hailey. Why would that change now?"

"I'm not sure. To spite me? And with her moving to Boston, I'm just…worried."

"Know what helps me when I get stuck in my head?" Jonah said. "Physical activity." He nodded toward the door. "There's a couple of trees we can clear from the woods out back, chop them into firewood."

"Sure," Devin replied. He liked chopping wood. It was both repetitive and satisfying. And the space he'd cleared for woodcraft, where they'd be doing the chopping, was pretty nice, if he did say so himself.

"All right." Jonah cuffed him on the shoulder. "And maybe then you can tell me why my sister's face goes red every time you've come up in conversation lately."

Cassie was already in a booth at the bakery when Alex arrived. She moved Tyler's high chair out of the way so her brother could slide in across from her. He ruffled Tyler's hair after he propped his cane against the end of the bench and got settled.

"Have you ordered?" Alex asked, glancing at her coffee cup, which was half-full.

She shook her head. "Waiting for you."

"Do you know what you want?"

"A turkey sandwich. I need protein."

He lifted his hand to get the waitress's attention. Cassie ordered first, then Alex asked for what he always got here, regardless of the time of day: a fried cranberry muffin and a side of crispy bacon.

"So," he said, sitting back and sipping the orange juice Cassie had ordered for him before he arrived. "I wanted to pick your brain."

"About…?"

"Adoption."

She cocked her head to the side. "What about it?"

"What do I need to do if I want to get the ball rolling on adopting a child out of foster care?"

"Alex." She sat back, stunned. Tyler dropped a piece of his half-eaten rice rusk onto the tray of his high chair, then started smearing it all over the tray. "What?"

"Look, I know it might sound crazy, but that kid—Parker. I've been thinking about him all week."

"I felt bad for him, too, but adoption is a huge deal, and that boy needs a lot of care. You're only twenty-three and you're basically working two jobs right now: your job at the retirement community and your job at camp. How are you going to give him the time and attention he needs?"

"The camp stuff's not a big deal—it's part-time at best," he said. "And lots of people have kids by the time they're twenty-three."

"But not when they're single—"

"You're single."

"—and it's a special needs child."

"Don't you see, though, Cass? His special needs are *my* special needs. I get this kid. I could have been this kid. But I wasn't, because I had Mom and Dad to help me. He doesn't have that right now, but I think… I think God's calling me to be that for him."

Cassie squinted at her brother because…that's exactly how she'd felt when she'd trained to become a foster parent. Called. "You've prayed about it?"

"That's practically all I've been doing since last weekend. I'm scared, Cass—it's a big deal, and I know it. But at the same time, I can't just ignore that this kid's out there when I'm pretty sure God wants him to be with me."

"Have you talked to Pastor Nate?"

"Twice, actually."

"What did he say?"

"The first time, he wanted me to sleep on it for a few days. Yesterday, he suggested I talk to you about your experience."

"Wow." Cassie wrapped her hands around her coffee cup, which was no longer hot, just warm. "This is a big deal."

"I know."

She glanced at Tyler, who gave her a wet smile, his first two teeth shining like little pearls. "There's always a chance it might not work out."

His gaze volleyed between her and the baby. "Have you

heard anything about the court case?" After finally getting a hold of her parents on the phone, she'd given her brothers a bare-bones update about what was happening with the man claiming to be Tyler's biological father.

"No."

"It'll work out."

She certainly hoped so, but she had her doubts. She pushed those to the side to focus on Alex and this monumental change he was thinking of making in his life. "Are you sure you're ready for this?"

A smile teased the corner of his mouth. "Throw me in the deep end. I'll learn."

She leaned forward in her seat. "All right, then. Do you have a pen? You're gonna want to take notes."

Chapter Sixteen

Devin hefted his ax up over his shoulder, then let it fall. *Thwack.* The blade cleaved through the log in front of him, cracking it in two.

He put the ax down and wiped a bead of sweat off his forehead. He and Jonah had been at this for quite a while now, and they had a healthy pile of firewood stacked up.

Jonah poured half a bottle of water over his head, then slicked the water out of his eyes. "You good?" he asked. "Or do you have more nervous energy you need to chop out?"

"I'm good." Devin gestured toward the water bottle. "Gimme that."

Jonah handed it over and Devin poured the rest of it onto his own head. "Ahh."

"Feels good, right? This right here is why I became a PE teacher. To help kids learn how exercise can help them manage their stress."

"And here I thought it was because you're just a big kid yourself."

Jonah grinned. "That too."

They both grabbed their axes and secured them in the shed, locking the door behind themselves when they came out.

Devin surveyed their handiwork. "What are we going to do with all this wood?"

"Stack it up behind the shed, then cover it with a tarp to

keep the rain off. The kids can use it when they're learning how to build fires."

"I thought we were going to make them collect kindling from the forest. Survival skills, and all that."

"We are." As the head counselor, Jonah had the final say on how they set up all the activity stations. "Doesn't mean we can't help them out with a log here or there if they need it. Especially the little ones, like Hailey."

Devin nodded. Fair enough.

They started carrying the wood over to the shed.

"So..." Jonah said after they'd dumped their first batch of logs into a pile, "my sister, huh?"

Devin sighed. He was still disappointed about how Cassie had shut him down after that kiss the other night. "Dude, do we have to?"

Jonah lifted an eyebrow. "Is there something to tell?"

"You asked, didn't you?"

"Yeah, 'cause I thought you were finally going to admit your big crush. Not because I thought you had tea to spill."

Devin massaged one of his temples. "What do you mean, finally?"

Jonah snorted. "Oh, come on. Tell me you haven't been crushing on Cassie since sixth grade."

Devin's face heated. He'd never told Jonah about his feelings for Cassie. Back then, his buddy would have laughed him out of the room. "Was it that obvious?"

"Oh, most definitely."

"Did *she* know?"

"Doubt it. You were a nonentity in her life back then."

"Great." He was pretty sure he was a nonentity in her life now, too.

"You looking to change that?"

Devin shrugged, then picked up another armful of firewood. "I don't think she wants me to."

Jonah frowned. "No, probably not."

Devin shot his friend a scowl. "Thanks for the vote of confidence."

"It's not you, bro. Her ex-husband burned her real bad. I don't think she'll be looking for another relationship any time soon."

The thought of that idiot—that idiot who'd been supposed to love, honor and cherish her—hurting Cassie felt like a punch to the gut. "He was a drinker, right?"

"Among his many other misdeeds."

"Did he cheat on her?"

Jonah sucked some air between his teeth. "Probably, but who knows? Let's just say that when we found out why he left her, my dad and Alex had to physically restrain me from driving up to Boston and giving that creep a piece of my mind."

"He didn't hurt her, did he? Physically, I mean?" Forget a gut punch; that thought made Devin feel like he was going to be sick.

"Like, hit her?"

"Yeah."

Jonah shook his head, leaving Devin baffled as to what the guy could have done to provoke such an extreme reaction from his friend. "Then what happened?"

"I shouldn't be talking about this. If she wants to tell you, she'll tell you."

"You can't dangle that kind of thing in front of me and then leave me hanging. Now I'm worried."

Jonah's eyebrows shot up. "You're *worried*?"

"Yes, okay? I like her. And you're making me worry about her."

"Aww, Dev." Jonah flashed him an impish grin. "You're adorable when you're lovesick."

"Don't be a jerk."

"Can't help it. You make it too easy."

"Yeah, yeah. Laugh it up. One day this'll be you, and instead of helping you, I'll laugh and tell you that you deserve whatever misery you're in."

"Bro," Jonah said, still grinning, "are you asking me to be your wingman?"

Devin rolled his eyes. "Dream on. You'd be the worst wingman in the history of wingmen."

"Hey! That's not true! I'd talk you up like a champ. And she's my sister, so she'd listen to me for sure."

"She'd listen to you all right. Listen to you tell all kinds of embarrassing stories about me from back in the day."

Snickering, Jonah drummed his fingers together. "There's just such a wealth of material to choose from…"

Devin barked out a laugh. "See? You'd send her running in the opposite direction."

"Seriously, though. You really do like her? For real? You're not just saying that to get a rise out of me?"

"I've always had a thing for her. And now that I know her better…"

His buddy held up a hand. "Say no more. I'm on it."

"Jonah—no. I seriously don't need you to be my wingman. And it's a lost cause, anyway. She's not into me."

"How do you know?"

"Because I've asked her out twice, and she's turned me down both times."

"Did she tell you why?"

Devin shook his head. "You said it yourself. She's not looking for a relationship right now."

"Anything specific about *you*, though?"

Devin dumped another load of firewood onto the pile behind the shed, thinking back to what she'd said the other night. "It sounded like she thought it would muddy the waters for us to continue working together if we started dating, and maybe it would confuse the kids, too."

Jonah tapped his chin. "Okay, so her hesitation might be about the situation as a whole, not necessarily something about you."

"Maybe. But she's seen me at my worst, so I wouldn't be surprised if she was just letting me down easy. And unless the camp fails, this situation isn't changing, anyway, so it's kind of a moot point either way."

"Let me do some recon, see if I can suss out whether your drunken teenage tomfoolery is a deal-breaker for her."

"No, don't do that. You'd make an even worse spy than a wingman. I'm just going to let it go. I don't want you to weird her out or make it any more uncomfortable for her than it already is."

Jonah rocked back on his heels and nodded in approval. "Gotta tell you, I'm digging this protective side of you for her. She needs that after everything she's been through. Someone who's going to put her first."

Devin studied his friend for a second, surprised. "If we started seeing each other, you'd actually…approve?"

"Why wouldn't I?"

"Because she's your sister?"

Jonah waited for a beat, then prompted, "And…?"

"And I'm not good enough for her?"

"Aren't you?"

"Considering I'm a single dad who wouldn't have a job or two pennies to rub together without your aunt, no, probably not. Oh, and I almost got her arrested for trespassing a couple weeks ago, so that probably counts against me, too."

Jonah's eyes bugged. "*Trespassing*? Where?"

"She didn't tell you about that?"

His buddy shook his head.

"It was the day we took Hailey kayaking and got caught in the rain. We took shelter on some lady's porch. She was in Boston but saw us on her doorbell camera and called the police."

Jonah laughed and did a facepalm. "Only you, man."

"It was the same cop who arrested me for driving under the influence back in school, so that was fun."

"I'll bet."

"Small towns have long memories. I'll always be the kid who was arrested for DUI."

Jonah shrugged. "Is that part of your past? Sure. Will there be some people who can't get over it? Probably, but so what? You're not that guy anymore. God knows that, and the people who know you know that, too. You're good enough for whatever it is you want out of life, Dev. If that's my sister and she wants you, too, then I say go for it. Seize the day."

Devin gave him the side-eye. "I'll be honest. I was expecting you to go all brother bear on me."

"You forget that she's my *older* sister. We never had that kind of relationship. I was like a little puppy nipping at her heels, not a guard dog." He held up a hand. "That said, if you *do* get together, ixnay on the PDA, all right? Otherwise, we might have to have words."

"Meh." Devin shrugged. "I could take you."

But he knew that if Cassie ever gave him a real shot, he'd do everything he could to gain her family's support and respect.

Cassie, Devin and Alex stood at the back of one of the conference rooms at Collingwood Place, the senior living community where Alex worked. There were several rows of chairs set up, but they were all empty. The talk was supposed to have started five minutes ago, and there were exactly zero other people in the room.

Cassie glanced at the two men beside her. "Tell me again why you guys thought this would be a good idea?"

Devin rubbed the back of his neck, a sheepish expression on his face. "Uh, because Walter said so."

"Walter, the septuagenarian DJ for the dance at the open house?"

"That would be the one."

She took out her phone and glanced first at the time, then at her brother. "How long do you think we should wait?"

"Give them a few more minutes."

"Really? You think someone will show?"

Alex smirked. "I think they're all going to show. But it's coconut cream pie night in the dining room, and who can say no to coconut cream pie?"

Within minutes, upward of thirty seniors trooped into the room. The last person in line clapped his hands as he entered. "Let's get this party started!"

Cassie's lips tipped up. This had to be DJ Walt.

Walter took a moment to shake hands with Alex, Cassie and then Devin. "How's my disco ball?" he asked.

"Glimmering away," Devin replied.

"Perfect." Walter took a seat up front. "So, tell us about your camp."

Alex stepped forward and started woodenly reciting the description they'd posted on the website. "Camp Piper is a summer camp for boys and girls located right here in beautiful Sandpiper Cove. Our programs center around environmental education and outdoor fun. At Camp Piper—"

"Not the canned spiel, Alex," Walter interrupted. "Tell us what it's really like."

Alex shot Cassie a panicked look. As an accountant, public speaking wasn't his forte, but since he knew all the residents here, they'd agreed that he should take the lead.

Now, however, her big-sister mode had been activated, and she rushed to help him out. "It's gorgeous," she said to the crowd. "We've got twenty-five acres of land, most of it woodland, but we also have access to Piper Marsh and Piper Beach, so the kids get to spend a lot of time exploring the beach and the wetlands in addition to the forest. They learn about marine biology through hands-on activities, they swim in our little kettle pond, they kayak, they learn survival skills for hiking and camping, and they have lots of fun playing sports, doing arts and crafts and learning new skills like archery, woodcraft and fishing."

There were a couple of oohs and aahs from the crowd. Then a small, silver-haired lady in the back raised her hand. "It sounds great, but isn't this a new camp? You make it sound like kids are already doing these things, but how could that be if you're just opening this summer?"

"That's a great question, and I'm glad you asked," Cassie said. "We're not actually opening this summer; we're reopening. My aunt and uncle built Camp Piper almost thirty years ago, and they ran it together for a long time before he passed away. My brothers and I all attended when we were growing up, so when I talk about the activities we have at camp, I'm speaking both from the camper perspective and from the director's perspective. Will we have a few new attractions now? Yes, we will. But the core experience will be the same as it always was, and that's to give kids a great summer full of fun and friendship while also teaching them new skills and fostering their independence."

The lady who'd asked the question nodded, satisfied. Another woman raised her hand. "Do you offer any adult or family camps?"

"Right now, we're still building out our off-season programming. We do host school groups in the fall, winter and spring, but if there's enough interest in an adult camp or family camp, that's certainly something we'd be willing to put together for you."

An audible ripple of interest ran through the room, and Cassie felt hope balloon in her chest. Registrations for the summer had been slow, but maybe there was a new market they could tap into here.

And maybe, like Walter had said to Devin and Jonah, the folks in this room would be willing to spread the word about Camp Piper to their families and friends.

Glancing over her shoulder, she caught Devin's eye, a jolt running through her as she remembered the way he'd looked at her the night they'd kissed.

Had Jared ever looked at her like that? Had *anyone* ever looked at her like that before?

Maybe if they didn't work together… Maybe if he wasn't living right next door…

But they did and he was and the worst part was that those weren't even the real reasons she couldn't afford to kiss him again. They were just the excuses she'd used so she wouldn't have to reveal how broken she was inside.

Chapter Seventeen

"Daddy," Hailey said, setting her backpack down on the kitchen table, "is my mom still in Boston?"

"She went back to Colorado, peanut. But she'll be back at the end of August. Why? Do you want to call her?" This was the first time Hailey had brought up Shannon since the hotel sleepover debacle, and although Devin had no desire to speak with Shannon right now, he'd do it for his daughter.

"No, we don't need to call."

"Are you worried about seeing her again? Because like I told you, you won't have to stay with her overnight anymore."

"No, I'm not worried."

"Why did you want to know if she's in Boston?"

"We're having a Mother's Day tea party at school."

"Oh." Similar school events had happened ever since Hailey had started preschool, and Devin hated that her mother was absent every year. "I'm sorry she won't be there. Do you want to ask Ms. Mirriam to go with you like she did last year?"

"I want to ask Miss Cassie."

Wincing inwardly, he asked, "Are you sure, honey bunny? Miss Cassie's busy with Tyler, and Ms. Mirriam had such a good time with you last year." Plus, it might not be the most considerate idea to invite Cassie to a Mother's Day event when Tyler's adoption status was still up in the air.

"Me and Miss Cassie are mermaid twins, Daddy. And it's a tea party, like my birthday! I know she'll want to go!"

"You can ask her, but if she says no, she says no."

"Okay," she said, skipping toward the front door. "Let's go!"

"Now? Don't you want to have an after-school snack?"

"I'm not hungry, Daddy. I want to ask her now!"

Devin sighed. He'd interacted with Cassie since the kiss, but it had been purely professional. She hadn't brought it up, and he hadn't, either. What was there to say? She knew where he stood, and she'd made her stance clear, too. Unless she changed her mind, they were at an impasse.

He wasn't holding his breath.

They went outside, and he immediately noticed an unfamiliar car parked outside Cassie's cabin. Huh. Most visitors parked in the parking lot—they didn't drive right up to the cabins on the little dirt access road the way he and Cassie did.

"It looks like she has guests," he said. "We should come back later."

Hailey sprinted ahead. "No, Daddy," she called out over her shoulder. "Now." She ran up Cassie's porch steps and started banging on the door. "Miss Cassie! Miss Cassie! It's me!"

"Hailey!" Devin jogged up the steps after her, grabbing her hand to stop her from knocking again. "I know you're excited to ask her about the event, but pounding and hollering like that isn't very nice, especially if she has visitors over."

"I want to ask her now, not later!"

"That's not up to you, Hailey. She's not answering the door."

"But she's in there, I know it! I can hear her talking."

Actually, now that they were standing right here, Devin could hear her, too. He couldn't make out any distinct words, but she definitely sounded upset.

"She's busy, peanut. Let's go."

"No! Miss Cassie! Miss Cassie! Let me in!"

Hailey hadn't had a meltdown like this since her birthday. And that one, too, had taken place right here on Cassie's porch.

"Alley-oop," he said, scooping her into his arms, throwing her over his shoulder and carrying her back down the steps.

"Daddy!" she screamed, slamming her little fists into his back. "Put me down!"

"Hailey?" The sound of Cassie's voice stopped Devin in his tracks. "What's going on?"

Devin turned and set Hailey back on her feet. Cassie's eyes were red, her face swollen from crying. In the background, he could hear Tyler crying, too.

"You look busy," he said, his stomach falling to his feet at the unhappiness on her face. "We'll come back later."

"Miss Cassie!" Hailey cried, oblivious. "I need to ask you something!"

A woman Devin had never seen before appeared in the doorway, holding Tyler, who was bawling. "Okay," she said briskly. "I think I've got everything."

"Please don't do this," Cassie said, reaching for the baby. "At least give me some time to say goodbye."

"I'm sorry," the woman said. "I'm on a tight schedule. We have to go."

"Muh, muh, muh," Tyler cried, arching toward Cassie.

Her face crumpled as she kissed the side of his face, tears dripping from her chin to his shoulder. "Goodbye, sweet boy. I love you."

"What's happening?" Devin asked, feeling lost and powerless.

Cassie just shook her head, the tears still falling, as the woman marched a screaming Tyler down the steps and strapped him into her car.

"Who is that?" Devin demanded, ready to intervene, if necessary. "Where's she taking Tyler?"

"Tyler! Tyler! Don't cry!" Hailey ran toward the car as the

strange woman slammed the door on the red-faced, screaming baby.

Cassie was crying too hard to answer, so the woman gave Devin a businesslike look and explained, "I'm Tyler's caseworker. We're moving him to a new placement."

Devin whipped around to Cassie. "Can she do that?"

But by then, the caseworker had already started the car.

"Tyler! Tyler!" Hailey cried. They could still hear him screaming, even over the sound of the car as it started driving away. "No! Daddy! Where's he going?"

"Away, peanut," he said, disbelief turning the words as thick as tar on a hot day. "She's taking him away."

Cassie was wrapped in a blanket in front of Devin's fireplace. She was still in shock.

Devin had steered her over here right after the caseworker had driven away. It had taken a while for Hailey to calm down, but she'd finally quieted and was now in bed. Cassie had heard Devin comforting her, but she hadn't participated. She couldn't. Now that Tyler was gone, she could barely move.

Devin came into the room and added another log to the fire, which was roaring. It wasn't particularly cold, but the flames gave Cassie something to look at, something soothing and hypnotic that didn't require any mental concentration, and she was grateful he'd thought to make one.

He brought a mug over to the coffee table in front of her, then sat in the armchair next to the sofa. "I made you a hot chocolate. Tea might've been better, but we don't have any."

Cassie reached for the cup. "Thanks." Her voice sounded flat even to her own ears. He'd offered to call her parents, Aunt Mirriam or her brothers for her, but she'd told him not to. She couldn't face telling anyone else what had happened right now.

She took a sip of the hot chocolate. The warmth was nice

and the chocolate was delicious, but swallowing felt like a chore. She set the mug back down, staring into the flames.

A few minutes later, Devin asked, "So, they're allowed to remove kids from the home whenever they want to? No notice needed?"

Cassie swallowed thickly. She was all cried out. "When she told me about the court case, she warned me. I didn't want to hear it."

"What happens now? After the DNA test? Do you get him back if it's not a match?"

She shook her head, still staring into the flickering flames of the fire. "I doubt it. She said that I'm too emotionally invested. That I'm putting my needs over the needs of the child."

"That's ridiculous," he said. "You can never be too emotionally invested in your child."

A tiny spark of...*something*—respect, maybe, or admiration—made her look up briefly from the flames. He was a good dad. Say what you wanted about his teenage arrest record and his rash and irresponsible marriage, but Devin Spencer had turned his life around for his little girl. He was a family man through and through.

"Jared and I tried for a baby for years. Never happened."

"I'm sorry," he said, his tone tentative. "Did you try getting tested to see what the problem was?"

She gave a bitter laugh. "Did we ever."

He waited, and she decided to throw caution to the wind. They were never going to be an item, anyway. He might as well know the ugly truth.

"When we were dating, we both said we were saving ourselves for marriage. Turns out only one of us was telling the truth."

She turned her eyes back to the fire, but she could still feel his gaze—patient, steady, unwavering—on her face. "He gave me an infection that had no symptoms, so it went untreated for a long time. By the time the doctor caught it, it had caused a lot of internal damage and scarring. Too much," she said, her voice dropping to a whisper, "for me to ever have a baby of my own."

"Aww, Cass." He leaned forward in his seat, his eyes crinkled in concentration and concern. "I'm so sorry."

"And after all that, I forgave him. We were married, and people make mistakes. He said he lied because he was scared to tell me, scared he'd lose me. So I prayed about it. I went to therapy, I went to Al-Anon. I begged God to let me be at peace with him and the whole situation, and I got there. I forgave him and let it go."

She took in a deep, shuddering breath. "But when I started talking about adoption, he got cagey. Going through an adoption agency is expensive, and he said he wanted to work for another year or two at his surgeon's salary to save up for it. And I believed him *again*."

The fire popped, and Devin's mouth etched an unhappy line on his face.

"When he handed me the divorce papers, I was completely blindsided. I thought we were in a good place, or at least that we were making it work. But his drinking ramped up a lot after we learned about my infertility, and he said it was because the guilt was eating him alive. Even though I'd told him a million times I'd forgiven him, he didn't believe me. He also said he couldn't picture going through life without having biological children. He'd tried to accept it, tried to accept *me*, but he couldn't. He had to be 'true to himself.' He had to leave and find a woman who could give him the life he'd always dreamed of."

Devin made a sound that was halfway between a snort and an exclamation of distress.

"And when I flipped out and told him that I could have given him that life if he hadn't lied and infected me, he shrugged and said he couldn't change the past but he *could* change the future. So that's how I ended up here. Divorced. Infertile. And—" her voice cracked "—now that Tyler's gone, alone."

She'd thought all her tears were spent, but they weren't. They were clogging her throat, blurring her vision and running down her cheeks *again*.

She buried her face in her hands and wept. For herself. For Tyler. For all the dreams she'd had that had turned to dust.

The sofa shifted as Devin moved from the chair to the couch. "Hey now," he murmured, wrapping her up in his arms and drawing her to him. "I'm here. You're not alone."

For a fleeting moment, as she cried into his strong, sturdy chest and breathed in his smoky, woodsy scent, she even let herself believe it might be true.

Care, support, acceptance—it was all *right here*.

But when she finally stopped crying, looked up and leaned in, hoping for a kiss, he gently pushed her away.

Love was no longer in the cards for her. The damage Jared had done was irreversible, and it would always, *always* have the final say.

Chapter Eighteen

Devin pulled into the school parking lot and turned around to face Hailey. "Are you sure you don't want me to come in?"

"Daddy, it's a *Mother's Day* event. For mothers. Not you." He almost laughed at her tone of voice. She was seven going on seventeen with all that sass.

"I know, peanut, but since you didn't want to ask Ms. Miriam—"

"I asked Miss Cassie. She said she'd come."

Devin rubbed the back of his neck, worried. He'd tried to call Cassie to confirm that she'd show up for this, but she was ignoring his calls. Ignoring his texts, too. And she wasn't staying at her cabin right now, so he hadn't even seen her over the past few days.

He needed to talk to her. Not just about this Mother's Day event for Hailey, but about everything they'd talked about the other night. The huge secret that she'd shared.

He'd seen the look in her eyes when they were sitting together on the couch. He knew she'd wanted to kiss him.

He wanted that, too, but not like that. Not right then.

He'd been far too careless with women in the past, and he'd made a promise to himself when Hailey was born that he'd never be that careless again.

And this was Cassie they were talking about. Not just any

woman—*the* woman. The woman he loved, the woman he wanted to spend his life with.

He didn't want to kiss her to distract her from the sorrow of losing Tyler or the betrayal of her ex-husband or the bitterness of her divorce.

No, when he kissed her, he wanted it to be pure—he wanted it to be all about the two of them. Their past, their present and, God willing, their future, too.

"Well, I haven't heard from her, so I'm not sure—"

"There she is!" Hailey cried, flinging open her door and pointing. "Right there! I told you so!"

Relief hit him hard. She was here. She was okay. She wasn't flaking out on Hailey the way Shannon always did.

He got out of the car and raised his hand in greeting. "Hey."

She gave him an inscrutable look before turning her attention to Hailey. "Hi there, cutie," she said, bending down and opening her arms for a hug. "Are you excited for the tea party?"

Hailey flung herself at Cassie. "It's going to be so fun! We're doing a song and a dance and everything!"

"Sounds fantastic." Cassie straightened and held out her hand. "Lead the way." Hailey grabbed it and started pulling her toward the school entrance.

"Wait," Devin said. "Cassie, can we talk?"

She glanced back at him, that same indecipherable expression on her face. "Not right now, Devin."

"Later? I can meet you at the bakery after this. Say, ten o'clock?"

She shook her head. "I'm busy."

Disappointment descended like a fog. "Are you going to be home later? At the cabin?"

"I'm staying with Aunt Mirriam for now."

There were only a few days left before the open house and

the dance. She had to be extremely upset with him to move herself completely offsite. "Why?"

"Sorry," she said, not looking him in the eye. "We've got to go. We don't want to be late."

"Can I call you?" he asked, feeling worse and worse about where things stood between them with every passing second.

"Sure," she said, but she wasn't smiling, and she still wasn't looking him in the eye.

"Will you answer?"

She lifted her shoulder. "I've got a lot going on right now."

If that wasn't a polite brush-off, he didn't know what was.

Cassie plastered a smile on her face to greet Lisa and the other mothers from Hailey's class. She could do this. She could. So what if these other women had everything her heart desired? Life was what it was, and it wasn't always fair.

Lord, please take care of Tyler, wherever he is. Hold him in the palm of Your hand.

Besides, she was doing this for Hailey, who'd been given a raw deal herself, with Shannon as her mom.

"Great to see you here," Lisa whispered, squeezing Cassie's forearm as she sat down beside her in the row of chairs that had been set up for the moms.

"Hailey asked me to come since her mother can't be here."

"Of course she did. She talks about you all the time when she comes over to play with Avery. You're important to her. She loves you."

Cassie laid her hand over her heart. It both hurt and healed to hear that. "You think so?"

"I know so." Lisa smiled. "Heard her say it myself."

Pastor Nate had once said that, for a child, *love* was spelled T-I-M-E. And she and Hailey had certainly spent a lot of time together over the past couple of months. But it wasn't just about time for Cassie—it was also about Hailey's sweetness, their shared laughter and the little girl's trust. "I love her, too."

If she couldn't be a mother, at least she could be a friend.

The kids came out and did their song and dance. Then they served their moms a mini muffin and a tiny paper cup of lukewarm herbal tea. At the end, they presented each mom with a gift bag, and the teacher instructed them to open it together on Mother's Day.

Cassie bit her lip. "Do you want me to mail this to your mommy in Colorado for you?"

"No," Hailey said simply. "It's for you."

"Are you sure?"

"Mm-hmm." She lowered her voice to a whisper. "It's a drawing. My teacher said to draw us and our moms, but I drew me and you."

"Thank you, sweetheart. That means a lot to me."

"I'll come over so we can open it together!"

"I'm not staying at my cabin right now, honey." Mother's Day was this Sunday, and Cassie had no intention of moving back to Camp Piper until right before the first session of camp began in July.

If the first session of camp began in July.

"Oh, okay. Then you can bring it when you come over to see me!"

"On Mother's Day?"

"A course!"

Cassie really didn't want to go back to the site of her utter humiliation any time soon, but...she'd do it for Hailey. Because she loved her.

And when you loved someone, sacrifice was the name of the game.

Chapter Nineteen

Devin was chopping firewood again. He didn't know what else to do.

In hindsight, it was clear he shouldn't have let Cassie leave the other night without talking things through.

But she'd just had her worst nightmare come true when the social worker had shown up and taken Tyler, and he'd been trying to be a friend. Someone she could lean on. Not someone who made demands or forced her to talk things to death or refused to give her time alone to grieve her gut-wrenching loss.

No, when she'd gotten up after their almost-kiss and said she needed some space, he'd let her go. And now she wasn't even giving him the chance to explain why.

Putting the ax down, he took a swig of water and wiped his sweaty brow. It was almost seventy degrees today—unseasonably warm for early May. He collected an armful of the wood he'd cut and relocated it to the tarp behind the shed, the rich, mossy aroma even more fragrant when it was all piled up.

Someone cleared his throat behind him, and Devin spun around fast. "Jonah, you—" He stopped abruptly when he realized it wasn't Jonah who'd come to find him. It was a trim man in his fifties, someone whom he'd never thought he'd see again in his life.

"I heard the sound of the ax and took it upon myself to explore," Jack Campbell said succinctly. "I hope you don't mind."

Devin wiped his forehead again. "No, sir," he managed to spit out. "I don't mind, but I'm hardly fit for company right now." Whereas Jack looked ready to step onto a sailboat in tailored khaki slacks and a blue polo, Devin was a sweaty mess.

Hardly how he'd wanted to meet Shannon's father again, but there was nothing he could do about it now.

He could remember their first meeting with perfect clarity. Jack had shown up at his dorm room in a suit and tie, his fury evident from the hard lines on his face. A lawyer and a notary had trailed in his wake, presenting Devin with a plethora of paperwork to sign right then and there.

At the time, he'd treated the whole thing like a joke: the hasty, irresponsible marriage, the visit from his enraged father-in-law, the swift dissolution of the ill-begotten bond he and Shannon had shared.

Two months later, when Shannon had informed him she was pregnant, she'd told him in no uncertain terms that she didn't want her father to know. At that point, understanding that actions had consequences for maybe the first time in his life, Devin had nodded. "There's no way he'll hear about it from me."

Now, in the woods, he pulled at the collar of his shirt while Jack gave him an assessing look. "It's honest work, chopping wood. Must admit I've never tried it myself."

Devin half wondered if he should offer to give him a lesson, but decided against it. Whatever Jack was here for, it wasn't to learn proficiency with an ax. "What can I do for you, sir?"

"Jack," the other man corrected him.

Devin tilted his head in acknowledgment. "Jack."

"I understand you and my daughter have been keeping something from me. Or, I suppose I should say, someone."

Devin's stomach dropped. *Hailey.* Shannon had looped her father into it, just like she'd threatened to that night at the hotel bar. Jack's lawyers were probably waiting back at his car. Well, Devin wasn't the reckless, impulsive idiot he'd been back then. Those lawyers would be waiting a long time if they expected him to sign anything today.

"Jack, I—"

The other man held up his hand. "I'm not angry, not with you."

"Sir—"

"I'd like to meet my granddaughter, if that's okay with you."

Devin stared at him for a moment, this softer, gentler version of Jack failing to compute. "You should know, if you brought paperwork with you, I'm not signing anything. You'll have to send it to my attorney." The attorney he'd hire as soon as Jack drove away.

The other man held out his empty hands, palms up. "No paperwork, no lawyers. Just me."

"Why are you here?"

"I didn't know about her, about Hailey. Shannon never told me, not until a few days ago."

Devin continued to stare.

"My wife passed when Shannon was very young. I've remarried and divorced twice, but Shannon's my only child. If I'd known I had a grandchild—"

"That was Shannon's decision, not mine."

"I understand that," Jack said, his voice level. "Like I said, I'm not angry with you."

"Are you here because she wants custody? Because unlike the last time we met, I have absolutely no intention of giving in to your demands."

Jack shook his head slowly, an expression that looked a lot like respect on his face. "She doesn't want custody. She's not even moving to Boston anymore. Her current hospital in Colorado made her an offer she couldn't refuse, and she's decided to stay put."

Devin didn't know why he had mixed feelings about that.

Given what had happened during that sleepover, given the threat she'd made, he should be glad she was staying on the other side of the country.

He wasn't, though—not entirely. Despite everything, she was still Hailey's mom, and he didn't want his little girl to grow up without a mother.

"So you're here because…?"

"Because she's my granddaughter, and I'd like to know her."

"That's it?" Devin asked suspiciously. "You're not going to try to take her away from me?"

Jack's lips twitched with humor. "I'm fifty-eight years old. My child-rearing days are long behind me."

"There's always nannies." Like Shannon had told him. "Or boarding school." As Shannon had experienced growing up.

"I'll level with you, Devin. When Shannon came to me when you were both in college and told me she got married, I looked into you. Background check, PI on your tail, the works. And what he found? Let's just say I was not impressed."

Devin wanted to be offended, but he wasn't. He hadn't been impressive back then. He'd been a careless, partying punk.

"When she told me about Hailey, I did the same thing. But this time? I saw something different. I saw a man who'd cleaned up, who'd taken responsibility. Someone who was trying his best to give his daughter a great life. I know what that's like, and I respect it."

He held out his hand, and Devin, after a long moment, shook it.

"I'm only here because I'd like to meet her. There's no lawyers, no custody fight, no ulterior motives. I'd like to be her grandfather, if you'll let me."

Devin had never dreamed he'd see the day where Jack Campbell was humbly asking *him* for anything. If God could soften Jack's heart toward him, He could truly do anything.

"She's at school right now, but maybe, if you don't mind

waiting, we could meet you for dinner somewhere tonight." It would delay the conversation he needed to have with Cassie, but Jack had come a long way for a chance to meet the granddaughter he should have known all along.

Jack's whole face lit up. "I'd like that," he said. "A lot."

Oddly, Devin thought he might like it, too. Jack might not be his family, but he was Hailey's. The wider the circle of people who cared about his daughter, the better. Hailey deserved all the love in the world.

After she said goodbye to Hailey, Cassie stopped at Sandpiper Sweets and picked up lunch for her and Aunt Mirriam: two turkey and swiss cheese sandwiches on toasted croissants with a couple of cream cheese brownies for dessert.

Aurora wasn't behind the counter, which was a good thing. She'd for sure have been able to tell that something was wrong, and Cassie didn't have the energy to launch into the story of losing Tyler all over again. Calling her parents on their cruise, and then telling Aunt Mirriam and her brothers in person had been bad enough.

And then, of course, there was Devin, who'd been right there to witness it all.

Although he'd offered comfort at first, telling her she wasn't alone, ultimately he'd rejected her, then stood back and watched while she walked out the door.

Just like Jared.

So, yeah. If she wasn't keen on talking to him, if she wasn't keen on taking his call, could you blame her? She'd been more vulnerable with him than she'd been with anyone, and it had only reinforced what she'd already known: putting your heart in a man's hands was asking for trouble. Sooner or later he'd crush it—crush *you*—without a second thought.

Her chin wobbled, and she tightened her hands on the steering wheel, forcing herself to focus more on the scent of her toasted croissant sandwich than the emotions she had spinning around inside.

When she got to Aunt Mirriam's, she let herself in the back door. "I'm back," she called out, "and I brought lunch!"

Aunt Mirriam bustled into the kitchen, her hair in a loose bun. Today, she was wearing red jeans and a white V-neck, pulling off the look with effortless ease. "Ooh, what did you get us?"

Cassie handed the takeout bag over with a flourish. "Comfort food."

Her aunt smiled. "Good. You deserve it." Then she took two of her good china plates out of the cabinet, the plates with the gold trim and a pattern featuring pale pink roses, and started setting the table.

Cassie poured them each a water from the jug in the fridge while Aunt Mirriam folded their napkins.

"There," her aunt said, plating their sandwiches, then sitting and taking a moment to appreciate the sight of the pretty table. "Doesn't that look nice?"

"You didn't have to break out the good china for me."

"Oh, honey. Who else would I break it out for? Besides, sometimes it's the little things that can turn your whole day around."

Cassie thought about that for a moment, realizing it was true. The beautiful table, the anticipation of a good meal, her aunt's company—all of it did make her feel better.

They said grace and started eating. "How was the event with Hailey?"

"Cute," Cassie said. "Those kids are adorable."

"And being with the other moms…?"

Cassie sighed. "Hard. I mean, I'm happy for them, but…"

"You want what they have."

Cassie nodded. It was true. She was jealous. She wanted a family, too. "When Leah ran away," she started, then hesitated, because this was something Aunt Mirriam never talked about. "I mean, Tyler was only with me for seven months, and losing him is the worst thing that's ever happened to me. Worse even than what Jared did, or the divorce."

Aunt Mirriam placed her hand on Cassie's forearm and gave her a gentle squeeze. "God has a plan, honey. You have to believe that."

"I know. And I do. But it's still hard. And I really want to understand *why*."

Aunt Mirriam sat back in her chair. "You might not ever understand, and you have to make your peace with that. If you don't, trust me, it can take over your whole life."

Cassie blinked. This was the first time in years that she'd heard her aunt say she struggled with the loss. "Were you able to do it? Make peace with the fact that Leah ran away?"

"I try, honey. Every single day, I try."

"Even after all this time?"

Her aunt lifted her shoulder. "Five years—it's not that long."

The few days since Tyler's social worker had removed him from her home seemed like an eternity. Cassie couldn't imagine feeling devastated like this for another *five years*.

"Did you ever hear from her again? I know you and Uncle Vince tried so hard to find her while he was still alive, but… after that, did you ever find out what happened?"

"She talked a lot about the entertainment industry, so we flew out to Hollywood a few times, hoping to track her down, but nothing ever came of it."

"And she's never contacted you?"

Aunt Mirriam slowly shook her head. "I think the idea of an adoption started to scare her. She'd been on her own for such a long time."

Cassie's forehead furrowed. "I thought she *wanted* you to adopt her."

"She did. At first. But it's not uncommon for foster children to get cold feet about it when the day starts to approach. Vince and I both thought that's why she ran."

After mulling that over for a long moment, Cassie asked, "Did you ever think about fostering again?"

"Vince and I did talk about it, but then he passed and the idea of it just…overwhelmed me. But there are times…" She wrung her hands in her lap. "Are *you* thinking of doing it again?"

"Not right now, not when everything's still so raw. But maybe one day I could do emergency placements. They're shorter, and I'd know going into it that there's no chance I'd be able to adopt, so maybe I wouldn't get as attached." And maybe the sky was green and the sun was wet and macarons were her least favorite cookie of all time. But a girl could hope, couldn't she? Even if she was scared to let herself care that much for a child again, Cassie knew there were a lot of kids in need out there, and she still had a lot to give.

"Have you thought about going through an agency?"

Cassie wrinkled her nose. "I have, but it's so expensive." If they were able to open Camp Piper this summer and her income was stable, maybe she'd look into contacting an agency again.

"Didn't you get any money from the divorce?"

"Not really. We didn't have much saved because his student loans were so high."

"What about alimony?"

"I didn't want it. I just wanted out of the marriage as quickly and as cleanly as possible, so I said no when the mediator asked if I was going to push for it or not."

Aunt Mirriam pursed her lips. Cassie had finally shared the whole story of the divorce with her yesterday, so her aunt knew that Jared hadn't just left because Cassie was infertile—he'd left because he'd *caused* her infertility, and he couldn't get over the guilt. "You should have pushed. You deserved it."

Cassie shrugged, then got to her feet. Now that her secret was out there, she was done with that part of her life—truly done—and she just wanted to move on. "There's a few things I should do before the open house."

"Things you can do by yourself, or…?" Aunt Mirriam asked hopefully. Although she hadn't come right out and said it, it was clear to Cassie that her aunt hoped she and Devin might become more than colleagues, more than friends.

"Yes, by myself."

She could put on her professional hat and work with him when she had to, but if he tried to get personal, she was going to shut him down hard.

She didn't want to talk to him about the non-kiss, or the fact that she couldn't have kids. He'd made his position clear, and rehashing it—even if he was trying to let her down gently—would only make her feel worse.

Chapter Twenty

Cassie had opened the gates for the open house fifteen minutes ago, and they were still waiting for their first guests to arrive.

"Did you put the right time on the flyers?" she asked Alex.

He flashed her an irritated look. "You saw the flyers before we printed them. You proofread all the copy."

"Right. I'm just nervous, that's all. What if nobody shows up?"

"People are probably just sleeping in," Jonah said. "After all, it *is* Saturday."

Cassie chewed her lip. Sure, it was Saturday, but people got themselves out of bed on Saturday mornings all the time. The fact that nobody was here yet was a bad sign. A very bad sign.

The counselors they'd hired for the summer had been here for an hour. They were manning the various activity stations that would be open today: kayaking, hiking, sports, ecology and arts and crafts.

But if guests didn't start appearing soon, Alex might be forced to fire all of them. They still had a very pitiful registration roster for the summer, and if they didn't get more sign-ups today, they would likely have to call it on summer camp and focus their efforts instead on preparing for the school groups that would be coming in the fall.

Cassie could live with that. She had savings to fall back on for the next few months, and Jonah and Alex both had jobs, but what about Devin and Hailey? Obviously, living here at camp would go a long way toward relieving any financial shortfall, but the man would still have to buy gas and groceries, at the very least, not to mention his phone bill and car insurance and new clothes for Hailey, who was growing all the time.

If she were still in the process of adopting Tyler, she'd be even more anxious about today going well. But since she no longer needed to demonstrate job stability to social services, she at least didn't have to worry about that.

Devin and Hailey walked up from the marsh, where they'd been checking in with the counselors. When Hailey caught sight of her, she let go of Devin's hand and ran toward her like a hurricane. "Miss Cassieeeeee!" She launched herself at Cassie, grabbing hold of her waist. "Guess what?"

Cassie smiled down at her, trying to ignore Devin's presence completely. "What?"

"We had dinner with my grandpa last night!"

"Your grandpa?" Cassie repeated, throwing Devin a questioning glance. She knew his father had passed away before Hailey was born.

"Uh-huh," Hailey said happily.

"Shannon's dad," Devin added. "He dropped by yesterday afternoon. A total surprise."

Cassie blinked. "Wow."

"Yeah." Devin thrust his hands in his pockets. "Wow." The awkwardness was so thick you could practically swim in it.

Jonah waved toward the dining hall. "Alex and I are going to go make sure all the board games are set up." The forecast was threatening rain, so they'd decided to stock the dining hall with twenty different board games—chess, Monopoly, Yahtzee, Scrabble and lots more—in case the weather didn't play nice.

"Okay, good idea," Cassie said, waving them off.

"Will you give me a French braid?" Hailey asked, pulling at Cassie's hand. "I want to look nice for the open house!"

"Sorry, honey. We need to stay here and wait for people to show up."

"Can you do it here?"

Not wanting to disappoint the girl, Cassie quickly combed her fingers through Hailey's hair, then parted it into strands she could weave together. "Do you think my grandpa will like my braid?" Hailey asked.

"Is he coming today?" Cassie replied.

"He said he would for a little bit, but he can't stay for the dance. But that's okay because he's so nice! He got me ice cream!"

"That's great," Cassie said, wondering how it was that Shannon's father had come to visit them…and why. Was he planning to help Shannon pursue custody of Hailey? And if so, why didn't Devin seem more concerned?

"Ow! Miss Cassie! You're pulling my hair!"

"Oh, sorry." Cassie immediately loosened her grip, chagrined. But the idea that Devin might have to fight to keep Hailey, that Shannon might be able to sweep her away the same way the social worker had swept Tyler out of Cassie's arms…

It wasn't right. It just wasn't right.

Had Devin spoken to a lawyer yet? Had he saved enough money to hire one? If not, she could help. A lawyer wouldn't be able to help her get Tyler back, but she'd give up her savings in a heartbeat if it would help Hailey.

No question.

No hesitation.

No doubt.

She'd need a few minutes alone with Devin, though, to understand exactly what was going on.

"One of the girls in my class said it was weird that you came to our Mother's Day party, Miss Cassie, but I told her that was dumb. You're even better than a mother—you're a mermaid twin!"

Cassie's lips quirked up, despite the worry that had taken hold of her heart. "Thank you, honey, that means a lot to me. Mermaid twins are special, aren't they?"

"The specialest!"

She twisted an elastic band around the bottom of Hailey's braid. "Why don't you run into the dining hall to get a look in the mirror and see if you like your braid?"

Hailey patted the back of her head. "I love it!"

"You haven't even seen it."

"But I can feel it, and I love it!"

"I'm glad, but go take a look. I need a minute to talk to your dad about something."

"Okay!" Hailey said brightly, then scampered off.

Devin wasn't watching his daughter—he was watching her, his gray eyes glinting in the morning light. "You're really good with her."

Cassie didn't have the patience for small talk. "Have you hired a lawyer?"

Confusion flickered across his face. "What?"

"A custody lawyer. To fight Shannon."

"Oh. No. Shannon's not—"

A car honked as it made its way down the driveway from the gate toward the parking lot. And not just any car: a vintage red Corvette convertible with the top down and a happy senior waving like he was in a pageant or a parade.

Cassie and Devin both turned to stare. "Is that…?" Cassie started.

"Oh, it definitely is," Devin replied, laughing. "DJ Walt certainly knows how to make an entrance."

Just as Cassie was about to turn away and pick up their conversation where they'd left off, other cars started streaming in behind Walter. "Did he bring the whole retirement community with him?" she wondered out loud.

"Unless a bunch of them are driving minivans," Devin said, "I don't think so."

People started parking and getting out of their cars. And Devin was right: the majority of them were *not* seniors, but families with schoolchildren and young teens.

"Hiya, kids." Walter grinned as he walked over to them. "Like my ride?"

"It's a beauty, Walter," Devin said, shaking the older man's hand. "And you're like the Pied Piper."

Walter chuckled. "I try."

"Was everyone here following you?"

"Most of 'em."

Cassie looked back and forth between Walter and the cars still streaming in through the gate, flabbergasted. "But… how?"

Still smiling, he reached up and adjusted the brim of his corduroy cap. "Alex didn't tell you?"

"Tell us what?"

"I'm a bit of an online celebrity. An influencer, as the kids like to call us."

Cassie shook her head. Walter? An influencer? *What?*

"Like on Instagram?" Devin asked. "Facebook?"

"I have a radio show, actually, and quite the following on TikTok."

"TikTok?" Cassie repeated incredulously. "What do you do on TikTok?"

Walter winked at her. "I'm a DJ, hon. What do you think I do?" He did the moonwalk, then finished with a little spin and Vogue hands. "I dance."

Cassie couldn't help it—she laughed. She laughed and laughed until tears were streaming down her face and she could hardly stand up straight.

"You all right there, boss?" Devin crouched down beside her as she sat in the grass, succumbing to the weight of the hilarity. Walter, meanwhile, moved off to greet his many fans.

"He's a DJ," she gasped, wiping her eyes, "who dances—" she started laughing again "—on TikTok."

"Look." Devin held out his phone. "He showed me his TikTok handle while you were cracking yourself up."

She took the phone and scrolled. Walter had posted more than a hundred clips of himself, and he had almost a million followers!

"I guess you were wrong about social media," she said, looking around in awe. "Look at all the people he brought in."

He shrugged. "I thought Alex was off his rocker when he hired Walter to DJ the dance. Shows you how much I know."

"Now if we can just get some of these folks to sign up for camp..."

"They will," Devin said, holding out his hand to help her to her feet. "This place is great. I have no doubt."

She didn't want to let go of his hand, but she forced herself to do it. They weren't together. They'd never be together. He didn't want her anymore. "We should go make sure everyone's finding their way around."

"We should, but Cassie, we need to talk."

She looked away. "We don't, not right now." There were too many people around, and she needed to be in good form to help show Camp Piper to its best advantage. She couldn't do that if he poked at the pieces of her broken heart all over again. "Let's do it later, okay? After this is all over, and we know if camp's going to run this summer or not."

She could see that he was conflicted, but after a moment, he nodded. "Tonight, then, after the dance."

"And you don't need to go call a lawyer about Shannon and her dad?"

He shook his head. “Things there are all good, I promise. I’ll tell you all about it later, after the dance.”

If Hailey was truly safe and sound with Devin, Cassie would be happy, no matter how much the rest of their conversation might hurt.

Devin had been grilling hot dogs on one of the big outdoor grills for the last two hours, and the demand for them was finally winding down. Before the open house, he’d bought more than five hundred hot dogs from one of the big box stores near the country club in Chatsworth, and they were now down to the last pack.

“You’re sure one of us shouldn’t go pick up some more?” he asked Alex, who was cleaning up the table where they’d put the plates, napkins, condiments, pickles and chips.

His friend shook his head. “Everyone’s already eaten. We’d only need more for people coming back for a third or fourth dog.”

There was a pack of rowdy teenage boys who might well come back for thirds or fourths, but Devin would have no problem turning them away. They reminded him a little too much of his younger self, and he was determined to keep a close eye on them tonight.

He wiped his brow with his forearm. It was hot here by the grill.

“Finish what you’ve got cooking there,” Jonah said from the grill next to him, “and then we can sit down and have a bite ourselves.”

After they plated the last of the hot dogs, they took a seat at one of the picnic tables nearby. Music had been pumping out of the dining hall since dinner started, and everyone they saw coming and going seemed to be having a good time.

“Well,” Jonah said, crunching on a salt and vinegar chip, “we actually pulled it off.”

"Thanks to you, Alex," Devin added, throwing the man in question an amused glance. Without Alex, they'd never have gained a shoutout from DJ Walt.

Alex smiled. "I had nothing to do with that video he posted."

"Sure you didn't," Devin said, side-eyeing him. He fully believed Alex had invited Walt to participate in their festivities knowing that the man would champion their cause on his social media.

And indeed, the video in question had gone viral, bringing people to Camp Piper's open house not just from Cape Cod, but from all over New England—and a few from upstate New York, too. They'd had their hands full today, and as a result, their online registration system was bursting at the seams.

Not that Devin would get to enjoy the fruits of their labor, after all. He'd spoken to his former boss at the country club yesterday before he'd taken Hailey out to dinner with Jack, and he'd negotiated his old job back.

Well, not exactly his old job. Half of his old job.

His new job title would be co-director of the aquatics program, and he'd share the role with his boss's son, Lucas. Which Devin took to mean he'd do all the work, and Lucas would take most of the credit.

But whatever. It would be worth it if taking the job would clear the way for him to date Cassie.

He'd be taking a pay cut from what he used to make, too, although it wasn't as steep as fifty percent. Charles had offered him the job at eighty percent of his old salary, and Devin was going to take it.

He needed to prove to Cassie that he was serious about her, and that he'd do whatever it took to overcome the objections she'd made.

Jonah finished the last bite of his hot dog. "Where's Hailey?"

"She's been with your aunt since lunchtime."

Jonah grinned. "Aunt Mirriam to the rescue."

"Yup," Devin said. "As always." He glanced over his shoulder at the entrance to the dining hall, the sound of a disco song streaming out into the evening air. A thought occurred to him, and he looked back and forth between his two friends.

"What?" Jonah asked, wiping his cheek. "Do I have mustard on my face?"

"How old's your aunt?"

"Late fifties."

"And how old's Walter?"

Both Devin and Jonah turned to Alex, who frowned. "Nope."

"Come on, man. You don't know how old he is?"

"We're not setting my aunt up with Walter."

Jonah glanced at Devin. "I bet he's like seventy."

Devin shook his head. "He's probably only in his late sixties. Maybe even younger."

"Stop," Alex said. "We're not doing this."

"Not doing what?" Jonah asked innocently.

"They're grown adults. If they want to see someone, they'll see someone. We're not getting involved."

Jonah smirked. "Why so touchy, bro?"

"I'm not touchy." Alex scowled and folded his arms over his chest.

Jonah threw a quick glance at Devin. "He's touchy."

Devin nodded. "The touchiest."

Alex's scowl grew deeper. "You two are the worst."

"What's wrong with trying to bring someone a little happiness?"

"What you're more likely to bring them is humiliation and embarrassment."

Jonah raised an eyebrow. "When did a setup ever leave you humiliated or embarrassed?"

Alex looked away. "Drop it, J."

"Oh." Jonah sighed. "You're not thinking about a setup, are you? You're thinking about Leah again, right?"

Leah, as in Mirriam's runaway foster daughter Leah? Devin wondered. He wasn't exactly sure what they were talking about, but he *was* sure that this had gone beyond friendly teasing and Alex was now uncomfortable.

"We don't have to set them up," he said, standing as he caught sight of that rowdy group of boys coming out of the dining hall, scanning the scene and then laughing and high-fiving each other before trooping around the back of the building. "It was just a thought." He thrust his chin toward the boys. "You guys got things here? I'm going to go make sure those kids aren't getting themselves in any trouble."

"Yeah, we're good," Alex said. "Go."

Devin walked past the door to the dining hall. The music was pumping, kids were squealing and, when he poked his head inside, he could see that the adults milling around were having a good time, too. Some were dancing, some were snacking on chips and cookies, and some were just chatting and watching their children spin around the dance floor. Devin was pretty sure he even caught a glimpse of Officer Keeland, the police officer who'd given him grief during the rainstorm, although he couldn't be certain since the man wasn't wearing a uniform and he was dancing with a young girl who had to be his granddaughter.

Walter had taken off his signature corduroy cap to put his DJ headphones on, the strobe lights he'd brought turning the walls red, then green, then blue. Devin still couldn't believe how much he'd helped them. He'd never judge a book by its cover ever again.

He went around the side of the dining hall, where he could hear the boys he'd followed laughing, although he couldn't see them yet. They must be all the way in the back.

"Chug, chug, chug!"

When they started chanting, he broke into a jog. He could remember doing this exact kind of thing when he was a teen: sneaking a fifth of alcohol into a school dance and then meeting with some buddies outside to partake.

As he came around the back of the building, he saw that five boys had formed a loose circle around the sixth member of their group. They were still chanting as the kid in the middle lifted the bottle toward his mouth and—

"Hey!" Devin yelled.

The boys in the circle immediately took off, leaving the kid in the middle standing there alone, his eyes wide and scared.

"Put that down right now," Devin barked, nodding at the bottle.

The boy dropped it like it burned.

Devin picked it up, shaking his head in disappointment. "You don't want to do this, kid. Alcohol can get you into a lot of trouble, especially at your age."

"I'm sorry, mister. I-I was just going to have a little, I swear."

Devin sighed. "Are your parents here?"

"Don't tell them," the boy begged. "I didn't even take a drink."

"Sorry, kid. I'm a parent. I'd want to know."

"Th-they'll take my phone away. They'll ground me."

"Good. Actions have consequences. Getting grounded is a better way to learn that lesson than getting arrested. Let's go."

He marched the boy out from the back of the building, the bottle still in his hand. He was going to suggest to the parents that they get the boy to tell them the names of his friends, too. Devin was sure *their* parents would also want to know what their sons were up to.

If an adult had intervened earlier on his behalf, would his

path have been different? He wanted to think so, but he'd been stubborn. Convinced he knew better than everyone else.

As he and the boy rounded the corner, Devin stopped short when Officer Keeland took a look at the bottle in his hand and narrowed his eyes into slits.

Chapter Twenty-One

Cassie heard the commotion out front and went to investigate.

The police officer who'd confronted them the afternoon of the storm was staring at Devin with a hard look on his face. "Start talking," he said. "Fast." He wasn't in his uniform tonight—he'd clearly come to the dance as a private citizen rather than an officer of the law.

Devin held up a bottle of alcohol. "I caught some boys—"

"That's not true, mister," the boy next to him cried. "You brought that with you! You offered it to us!"

Shock, followed closely by panic, flitted across Devin's face. "I did no such thing."

"You did. You did!" the boy insisted. "Y-you said you'd give us five dollars each to take a drink from your bottle."

A few other people had gathered, and some of them murmured among themselves, shooting dark looks Devin's way.

This boy was going to get Devin arrested.

And Cassie knew there was no way on earth he'd ever do what this boy was claiming he'd done.

"All right," she said, stepping forward and staring the kid straight in the eye. "Let's go take a look at the security footage and see what it has to say."

All the color drained from the boy's face. "Th-there's cameras back there?"

"Yes," Cassie said succinctly, glad that Aunt Mirriam had insisted they install them when they revamped the camp.

"Timothy O'Donnell!" A middle-aged woman marched up to the little crowd. "What's going on here?"

"M-mom." He fisted his hands and rubbed at his eyes.

The woman eyed the bottle in Devin's hand. "Did you catch my son *drinking*?"

"Yes, ma'am," Devin said, "I'm sorry to say I did. Him and some of his friends."

Slapping her hands on her hips, she turned to her son. "Which friends?"

"Mom," the boy whined.

"Which. Friends?"

The boy named them, the real story of what had happened behind the dining hall coming out. Relief rushed through Cassie, alongside gratitude that the kid had backed down from his lie.

The boy's mother put a firm hand on his shoulder, then started steering him away. "Thank you," she said to Devin before she moved off. "I'm sorry they were causing trouble, but I appreciate you stepping in to protect them from themselves."

"Of course," Devin replied.

"What do you say, Timothy?" the woman prompted.

"Sorry," the boy muttered.

She glared at her son. "Say it like you mean it. Look him in the eye."

"I'm sorry," the boy repeated, louder this time.

Devin nodded, silently accepting the apology. Then he addressed the boy's mother. "I hope you'll let him come to camp this summer and make some new friends."

They moved off, and the other people who'd gathered to watch the confrontation, including Officer Keeland, filtered away, too.

Devin turned to Cassie and let out a long, shaky breath.

"Thank goodness you got here when you did. That could have gone very bad, very fast."

"I've got your back, Devin. I know you'd never do what he was saying you'd done."

"You didn't want to see the video footage first?"

She shook her head. "Didn't need to. I know you."

"Come here," he said, taking her hand. "Can we sit somewhere and talk?"

He led her down to the dock at the pond and they sat, their feet dangling into the water. Although Devin had taken his hand back to take off his shoes, he reached out again now and laced his fingers with hers.

She looked down at their hands, her heart racing, but she didn't want to read anything into it. She was afraid to get her hopes up. She didn't want him to crush her heart again.

"So," he said, "busy day, huh?"

She laughed a little at the understatement. "I'll say."

"Walter really came through for us."

"He sure did."

"Alex said registration is full, and you've even got a wait list."

Cassie nodded slowly, confused about why he'd just used *you* instead of *we*. "We do," she said pointedly, "and you're a big part of the reason why."

"I talked to my former boss. He's willing to give me my old job back."

Cassie gasped out loud. He couldn't leave. He was part of their team, and they needed him. "Why would you do that?"

His hand tightened around hers. "That night at the Cape Cod Grand, you said we had to think about what's best for the camp, and what's best for the kids. I can tell you right now that you'd be the best thing to happen to Hailey in a long time. She already adores you. If we started dating, she'd love you even more. And if you're worried about us working together at camp, I figured I could do something about that to try to clear the way."

Cassie opened her mouth, closed it. Opened it, then closed it again. "But—"

"If those were simply excuses, and you're just not that into me, it's fine. Just tell me. I can take it."

Not that into…? Was he insane? "You're the one who put me off when I tried to kiss you."

Sighing, he scrubbed his free hand through his hair. "I thought you might have taken that the wrong way."

She snatched her hand out of his hold. "What exactly was the right way to take it?"

"Cass." He laid his hand on her knee. It was warm. Heavy. Steady. "You were upset that night. I didn't want us to do anything you'd regret, and you'd been so adamant that you didn't want to go out to dinner with me."

She couldn't look at him. "I told you everything that night. Everything. Things no one else but me and Jared knew. And then…" She bit her lip, trying to stave off her tears.

"Hey," he said, moving his hand from her knee to her chin, gently turning her face to his and gazing deeply into her eyes. "It wasn't a *no* that night. It was a *not right now*. I'm glad you told me what happened with Jared. I'm glad you don't have to carry that all on your own anymore."

"But you said you want more kids and I can't—I mean, I'll never—"

He shook his head. "You think I only love you because of what you can give me? That's not how it works, Cass. I love you because you're you. That's it. The end. Full stop."

Her heart just about seized in her chest. She couldn't have heard him right. Love wasn't unconditional. She'd learned that lesson the hard way in her marriage. "What did you just say?"

"I said I love you. I'll do anything to be with you. Quit this job, move out of the cabin. Even with all the bad decisions I made in the past, you believe in me now. And you already love my daughter. Trust me when I tell you that those two things, they mean more to me than anything in the world."

Cassie closed her eyes. She was crying. Could she trust him? Was he for real?

"Don't cry," he said, wiping her tears away with his thumbs, then kissing where they'd trailed down her cheek.

"I miss Tyler so bad."

"I know you do, baby." He put his arm around her and drew her close.

"Even if he's better off with his father, or another family, I just want to see him again. I just want to know he's okay."

"I know. It's hard. I've been praying for him every day."

"I want a family. It's all I want."

He squeezed her tighter. "Be my family. Be Hailey's."

She wanted to say yes more than she wanted her next breath, but first, she had to know: "Will that be enough for you? If we can't have more kids?"

"You will always be enough for me," he said firmly. "But you should know that I'm adopted. It's why I fought so hard for Hailey when Shannon wanted to terminate the pregnancy. If you want children, I'm all in on fostering or adopting. I promise you, if you want a life with me and Hailey, we'll find a way to make all your dreams come true."

She took a breath. Her face was tingling where she'd been crying, but she didn't want to cry anymore. Hope was rising inside her like the first rays of daybreak after a long, dark night: orange, pink, gold and awe-inspiring. "Shannon's really not causing problems for you? Her dad wasn't here to intimidate you into giving Hailey up?"

Devin shook his head. "Nobody could ever intimidate me into giving up my daughter. And no, he was just here to meet her. Shannon hadn't told him about her until now." He filled her in on more of the story, and the worry she'd been carrying around all day finally disappeared.

"Don't take your old job back. Don't quit."

"Because you're not that into me and don't need to use that excuse anymore, or…?" he trailed off hopefully, faith, love and joyful anticipation shining in his gray eyes.

"Or I love you. And I trust you. And I want you to stay."

"Cassie." Love, longing, relief—she could hear all of it in the way he said her name.

"Devin."

"Kiss me."

She leaned in and obliged. Those colors she'd been seeing in her mind's eye—the pink, the orange, the gold—intensified into a kaleidoscope that left her breathless.

"You're good at that," he said, smiling when they broke apart.

"Well, I am a few years older than you," she said sweetly. "More practice."

"Oh, snap." He laughed. "So that's how it's gonna be, is it, boss?"

She smirked. "You started it."

"Me?"

"All that talk about respecting your elders, remember?"

"You're right." He shook his head. "But that's okay, it just means I'll need more practice." He pulled her closer and kissed her again.

"I'm sorry I was avoiding you."

"It's all right—I get it. I didn't express myself well, and you were hurt. But next time, tell me about it so we can work through it together, okay?"

She nodded and rested her head on his shoulder.

"You'll come over tomorrow for Mother's Day, won't you?"

She missed Tyler—she would always miss Tyler—but with Devin and Hailey by her side, she could find joy on even the hardest of days. "Alex, Jonah and I are taking Aunt Mirriam out for brunch, but I can come over later."

"It would mean the world to Hailey. And maybe next year, we can celebrate Mother's Day with you in a more official capacity."

"That'd be nice," Cassie said, meaning it.

And this time, when he aimed his crooked smile at her, it was clear that it didn't spell trouble after all. Instead, what it really spelled was…home.

Epilogue

Devin wiped his sweaty palms on his pants. It was the second week of August, and he and Cassie were walking back to their cabins after one of the nightly bonfires at camp.

The first season at the new and improved Camp Piper was going better than any of them had even imagined. The kids were having a blast, and the staff was, too. Cassie hadn't encountered any major medical emergencies in her capacity as the camp nurse, and Devin had floated around as a lifeguard, maintenance man and substitute counselor, filling needs as they arose. Hailey was as happy—and as deeply tanned—as he'd ever seen her. They were all sad that the summer was drawing to a close.

As he and Cassie neared their cabins, Devin grabbed her hand and tugged her toward the beach. "Where are we going?" she asked, stifling a yawn.

His heart raced. "Stargazing."

"Oh." She smiled. "I should have known."

They'd been doing this as much as they could this summer, coming down to the beach at night after their camp duties were done to walk along the shore. Some nights, the view of the stars was incredible. On others, clouds obscured how much they could see.

Sometimes, as they walked, they collected shells and sea

glass. More often, they'd take their shoes off and enjoy the feel of the sand and surf on their bare toes.

Tonight, Devin had a question he needed to ask her. It was fast, he knew it, but she'd contacted an adoption agency a couple of weeks ago, and he didn't want her going through the adoption process alone. Not when he and Hailey were ready, willing and eager to embark on that journey beside her.

He'd saved most of the money he would have spent on rent over the summer and earmarked it for a ring. He didn't have enough for a big diamond, but he'd found a beautiful blue opal in a bezel setting with three tiny diamonds on each side at the local jewelry store, and after conferring with Hailey—who'd agreed that a shiny oval opal was absolutely something a mermaid would wear—he'd taken the plunge and bought it.

It had been burning a hole in his pocket ever since.

At the beach, Cassie glanced left and then right. "Which way?"

He took her hand again. "Let's sit for a minute."

"Where?"

He led her to the end of the wooden boardwalk. "Here."

They sat, legs stretched out onto the sand in front of them. It was a warm night, humid, and the waves were calm. The moon was bright, letting him see her face clearly, but dimming the shine of the stars. "Everything okay?" she asked.

Once again, he wiped his palms on his jeans. "Yes, everything's great." How was he supposed to segue into this? He'd had a whole speech prepared, but now he couldn't remember any of it.

"Look!" She pointed up, and as he followed her gaze, a streak of light zipped through the sky. "A shooting star."

He smiled. Here was his opening. "Did you make a wish?"

She nodded.

"I did, too. Maybe you can make it come true."

She leaned her head against his shoulder. "What did you wish for?"

"That you'd marry me."

Her mouth fell open as she scrambled to meet his gaze. "Umm…was that a proposal?"

He grinned, adrenaline turning his nerves into a heady rush. "Depends, boss. If it was, would your answer be yes?"

Cassie pressed a hand to her heart in astonishment. "Devin! We've only been together for three months!"

"I've known that you were the one for me since I was twelve years old, Cass. I made a lot of bad choices between then and now, but somehow God saw fit to bring us back together and give us a real shot. If you'll have me, there's nothing I want more than to share my life with you and adopt babies with you and watch you French braid Hailey's hair every morning."

"Oh, wow. I—I don't know what to say." Cassie's eyes were wide as she pressed her hands to her face. "I'm shocked!"

He leaned over and kissed her cheek. "Say yes."

"Are you sure?"

"Positive." He took the ring out of his pocket and held it out to her. "Say yes."

She stared at it, her gorgeous brown eyes filled with wonder. "It's so beautiful."

"Hailey helped me pick it out."

He slid the ring onto her finger, where it gleamed in the moonlight. Then he gently kissed her on the lips. "Baby, please. I love you. I want to be with you forever. Tell me you want the same thing—say yes."

She gave a little gasp, as though only just realizing she hadn't answered the most important question he'd ever ask in his life. "Devin, yes! Of course I'll marry you. Yes, yes, yes!"

He crushed her to his chest, hugging her tight as he kissed her hair in joy and relief. "You had me sweating for a minute there."

She laughed, throwing her arms around his neck to hug him back. "I'm sorry! You shocked me! This is the biggest, best surprise of my life!"

"Stick with me, then," he said, winking before he kissed her again. "Because I'm pretty sure the best is yet to come."

The last Saturday in August had arrived, and the parents of the final few campers had just loaded their kids' duffel bags into their trunks and driven away. Against all odds, the camp had been completely full for both July and August, and many of the campers had cried before they left because they'd had so much fun.

The counselors were in their cabins, packing their bags, but Cassie, Devin, Alex and Jonah were all here in the parking lot, their hands still raised in their final goodbye waves.

"Well, team," Devin said, grinning as he dropped his hand. "We did it."

Jonah slapped Devin's back, then lifted Cassie off her feet in a bear hug. "We did it!" he crowed.

Alex gave them all a wry look. "One week until the first senior camp starts. Rest up while you can."

The first school group wasn't coming until the second half of September, but they'd decided to fill in the gap by hosting a four-day senior retreat over Labor Day weekend. The activities for the seniors would be a little different than the activities for the kids—hiking, painting and some longer bicycle trips would be the highlights for the older camp-going crowd. They were also renting a few vans so they could do day trips to a glassblowing museum, art galleries and, of course, a whale watching tour.

Walter and a few other residents of Collingwood Place were taking part in their inaugural senior weekend. They'd even convinced Aunt Mirriam to join the fun, although Cassie could tell that her aunt was a bit wary. She hadn't stayed onsite at Camp Piper since Uncle Vince had passed away.

"Let's go clean up," Devin said. "Cassie's got an appointment this afternoon."

"On a Saturday?" Jonah asked her. "Getting your hair cut or something?"

Cassie smiled. "Or something."

She wasn't really sure what her meeting was all about, to be honest. A few weeks ago, right before she and Devin got engaged, she'd decided to sign up with a private adoption agency. Last night, she'd received a message from a lawyer instructing her to meet him for coffee this afternoon. She'd thought it was odd, but she assumed it was somehow connected to the application she'd submitted to the agency. By the time she'd retrieved the voice message, however, the agency was closed, so she hadn't been able to get any clarity about the point of the meeting from them.

Jonah, Alex, Devin and Cassie helped the counselors clean, lock up and vacate the site. After her brothers left, Devin and Cassie got into her car. "You're sure you don't mind coming to this thing with me?" she asked.

"Given that you don't really know who this is or what they want, nope. Don't mind at all."

"We can get macarons for Hailey while we're there." The meeting was, conveniently, at Sandpiper Sweets, even though the adoption agency was located in Boston.

"Right," he said, winking and making air quotes with his fingers. "For Hailey."

She laughed. "Stop."

He grabbed her hand and kissed her knuckles. "You know I love your sweet tooth."

She laughed again. "Yes, because you know it means I'll leave your potato chips alone."

They drove to Sandpiper Sweets and went in. An older

gentleman in a suit stood up as they entered. "Cassandra?" he asked. "I'm Seth Warner. Thanks for meeting me today."

"Hello," she said, shaking his hand. "This is my fiancé, Devin Spencer. I asked him to join us." It still gave her a thrill to introduce Devin as her fiancé, and to see the beautiful, unique ring he'd given her on her finger.

The two men exchanged handshakes and pleasantries. "So," the lawyer said, "you must be wondering what this is all about."

"I presume it's connected with the adoption agency?" Cassie sat and pulled her chair closer to the table.

"Agency? No. I represent a private client."

"Oh," she said, confused. "But this is about an adoption?"

Seth smiled. "I hope so."

She shook her head. "I don't understand."

"I have a young pro bono client who came to me because he'd been in the foster care system for most of his life. He wasn't eligible for adoption when he was little—his parents would clean up for a few months to get him back, then return to their old ways once he was in their home again. The state finally terminated their rights a few years ago, but it's rare that anyone wants to adopt a teenager, so this client lived at a group home until he turned eighteen."

Cassie frowned. It was hard to hear about the cases where the system had let a child down. Plus, she really had no idea where this story was going, or what it had to do with her.

"He came to me a few months ago because he'd been dating a girl from the group home, but he lost touch with her when he aged out of the foster care system. When they reconnected, she shared with him that she'd had a baby—his baby—but she'd surrendered the child at a fire station."

Cassie's hand flew to her mouth. Tyler. He had to be talking about Tyler.

"This boy, my client, understandably did not want his child

in the foster care system. I tried to assure him that infants are almost always adopted quickly, but he didn't want to take the chance that the baby would be bounced around from home to home like he'd been, or end up in an otherwise bad situation. He wanted to gain custody so he could have a say in how—and where—the boy was raised."

"Is it—" Cassie could barely get the words out, she was shaking so hard. "Is the client you're talking about the father of my former foster baby, Tyler?"

The lawyer nodded. "Yes."

Cassie started crying, and Devin put his hand on her knee, letting her know that he was right here with her, that she could lean on him. She'd called Tyler's caseworker many times, trying to find out how he was doing, but the caseworker would always say that departmental policies and procedures wouldn't allow her to share any updates with Cassie.

Taking a breath, Cassie wiped the tears off her face. "Is he okay?"

"He's great. A beautiful, happy baby."

She sent up a prayer of thanks right away. She'd come to terms with the fact that she'd never learn how Tyler's story unfolded, but this right here? This meeting? This was a gift.

"Do you have a picture?"

"I can do better than a picture. Would you like to see him?"

Cassie gasped, looking all around the room. "He's here?"

"He's in the car with his father, a young man who wants to do right by him, but who also wants to take advantage of the scholarship he earned and finish getting his college degree. When he reviewed the records from DCF and saw that you'd been hoping to adopt Tyler, he wanted to reach out to you and see if you'd still be interested. Only this time, it wouldn't be through DCF, it would be through my firm. And he'd like an open adoption, so he can stay in touch."

The tears Cassie had been trying to staunch started flowing

again. "Are you serious?" If she'd thought Devin's proposal would be the biggest surprise of her life, she'd been wrong. Amazingly, gloriously wrong.

The lawyer's eyes crinkled as his lips tipped up. "Very serious."

"Of course I want him. And of course an open adoption works. Tell me what to sign and I'll sign it. Tell me your fee and I'll go to the bank right now."

"It's a pro bono case, remember? That means no fee."

"I don't—" She pressed her hand to her heart. "How? Why?"

Seth smiled sympathetically. "I was orphaned young myself. I know what it's like to be all alone in the world. Now that I'm semi-retired, I go around to all the group homes in my local area and talk to the kids there, let them know that if they ever need legal help, they can call on me. This young man did."

"I can't—I don't know how I'll ever thank you for this."

"It's not me," the lawyer said kindly, "it's Tyler's father who's making all the decisions."

Cassie nodded, even as her mind spun to figure out how she could support the young man who'd just turned her whole world upside down in the best possible way.

"We'll get to the paperwork later, but first, why don't you come with me?" Seth stood, and Cassie jumped to her feet.

Devin wasn't as quick to get up, and she turned a questioning glance on him. "You go," he said, his tone warm and encouraging. "Go see your son."

She held out her hand to him, refusing to leave him behind. They'd been talking about getting married at Christmastime, once her parents were home from their cruise, but if this was really happening, if she was really getting Tyler back, they'd need to move their timeline up considerably. They were a team now, and she wanted them to move forward with adopting Tyler together.

Everything, always, together.

The opal in her engagement ring glowed in the light as she waggled her fingers at him, urging him out of his seat. "One day soon he'll be your son, too."

Devin took her hand. He squeezed it. And then they both went outside together to greet the boy she'd loved from the moment she'd laid eyes on him, and to welcome him home.

* * * * *

Dear Reader,

Did you ever have the opportunity to attend summer camp? I did, in both the beautiful Canadian Rockies and the serene, forested wilderness of Ontario's Algonquin Park.

I learned many valuable lessons at camp—resilience, independence, teamwork and problem-solving chief among them. I think back on my days at camp fondly and often, which made it an absolute pleasure to dream up Camp Piper for this sweet little town on Cape Cod.

You'll see more of Sandpiper Cove and its inhabitants in my next book, which features Cassie's brother, Alex Reed.

But first, be sure to sign up for my mailing list at MeghannWhistler.com/newsletter for a special bonus scene showing what the future holds for Devin and Cassie. (Hint, hint—it's a wedding!)

Writing these stories for you brings me great joy. Please feel free to email me at Meghann@MeghannWhistler.com anytime!

Wishing you love and light,
Meghann